BACKSTAGE ROMANCE

"The play sure has been going well," I said.

Jason nodded, and then looked intently at me. I could feel his eyes pierce right through me. It was as if he were looking into my soul! He could probably even read my mind, which was silently screaming, "I am crazy about you, Jason!"

He moved closer to me. Maybe he *had* read my mind! My heart raced. I could hardly breathe. He was so close, close enough to kiss me. Maybe he *was* going to kiss me! What should I do? Should I keep my eyes open or close them if he kissed me? Some people say it's better with your eyes closed, but others say they like to see the moment as well as feel it.

Jason moved even closer.

This was it! This was the moment! I raised my face to his and slowly closed my eyes. . . .

Bantam Sweet Dreams romances
Ask your bookseller for the books you have missed

#1   P.S. I LOVE YOU
#174 LOVE ON STRIKE
#175 PUPPY LOVE
#176 WRONG-WAY ROMANCE
#177 THE TRUTH ABOUT LOVE
#178 PROJECT BOYFRIEND
#179 RACING HEARTS
#180 OPPOSITES ATTRACT
#181 TIME OUT FOR LOVE
#182 DOWN WITH LOVE
#183 THE REAL THING
#184 TOO GOOD TO BE TRUE
#185 FOCUS ON LOVE
#186 THAT CERTAIN FEELING
#187 FAIR-WEATHER LOVE
#188 PLAY ME A LOVE SONG
#189 CHEATING HEART
#190 ALMOST PERFECT
#191 BACKSTAGE ROMANCE

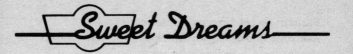

BACKSTAGE ROMANCE

Kelly Kroeger

BANTAM BOOKS

NEW YORK · TORONTO · LONDON · SYDNEY · AUCKLAND

RL 6, age 11 and up

BACKSTAGE ROMANCE
A Bantam Book / May 1992

ISBN 0-553-29453-9

Published simultaneously in the United States and Canada

Bantam Books are published by Bantam Books, a division
of Bantam Doubleday Dell Publishing Group, Inc. Its trade-
mark, consisting of the words "Bantam Books" and the
portrayal of a rooster, is Registered in U.S. Patent and
Trademark Office and in other countries. Marca Regis-
trada. Bantam Books, 666 Fifth Avenue, New York, New
York 10103.

PRINTED IN THE UNITED STATES OF AMERICA

OPM   0 9 8 7 6 5 4 3 2 1

To my mother,
June O'Connell,
who has inspired me through her writing

Chapter One

I stared at his gorgeous dark hair, wanting to reach out and touch it. His piercing eyes held mine, and his warm smile . . . I began to melt, and so did my chocolate Popsicle. It dripped down my hand, but I didn't care. I felt that the two of us were alone in the world.

My best friend, Beth, was a block ahead of me by now. "Krista, you've been staring at that picture forever!" she shouted.

"Just a minute," I said, waving at her from where I stood—next to the glass display case in front of the Community Playhouse. I moved over a bit so my reflection in the glass was right next to his photograph. My long blond hair contrasted with his dark locks, and my slender frame seemed lost next to his broad shoulders.

"You have ten seconds, Krista. Then I'm leaving," Beth warned.

I knew she wouldn't, but just the same, I gave Jason Stuart's picture one last lingering look. "Beth, will you come and see this musical with me?" I asked, licking a chocolate-covered finger.

She joined me at the display case. "Sure. Wow, he's good looking!"

Beth and I had been to almost every play and musical at the Playhouse. We were both big theater fans, particularly when gorgeous guys were involved. Beth had had a big crush on last summer's leading man in *Grease*. We must have seen the show seven times.

" 'The role of Bernard,' " I read in the caption next to Jason's picture, " 'in the musical *Summer Enchantment,* will be played by talented young Jason Stuart, a native of Morristown. Jason is a senior at Kennedy High School and plans to attend UCLA in the fall, majoring in Theater Arts. . . .' " Skipping down to the bottom, I added, " 'The show opens July fourteenth.' "

"I can't go with you," Beth moaned. "I'll be gone!"

I moaned, too. "What am I going to do while you're away?" I asked myself more than Beth. She would be at Camp Watanda for the entire summer as an assistant counselor, and I'd never spent a summer without her. I would have no one to hang out with, go

2

swimming with, see movies with. And the more I thought about it, the less I looked forward to the summer. *Oh, well,* I thought, *it's only May. We still have lots of time before Beth leaves.*

Just then the theater door opened and someone walked out. I froze, recognizing him immediately. "Beth," I whispered, "it's him!"

"Who?" she asked, much too loudly.

I grabbed her arm. "Jason Stuart! The guy in the picture," I hissed.

"Are you sure?" She craned her neck to get a better look, then raised her eyebrows. "Not bad—not bad at all."

"Careful!" I said, pulling her back. "He might see us." I took a quick peek. Jason Stuart was now sitting on a wooden bench near the theater door, holding a soft drink in one hand and a script in the other.

Beth's face brightened. "I know, let's ask him for his autograph!" she said mischievously.

I gasped. "You wouldn't dare . . . would you?"

A smile spread across Beth's face. I shouldn't have asked because I knew the answer. She marched right over to Jason, dragging me with her.

"Excuse me," she said to him.

Jason smiled up at us, and I felt my knees grow weak. He was *so* handsome!

"We were just wondering . . . well, actually

my friend here was wondering . . ." Beth took a piece of paper out of her purse. I held my breath, ready for complete and utter embarrassment.

". . . if you could tell us what time it is?" she went on, depositing her gum in the paper and stuffing it back in her purse.

"Why, sure." He glanced at his watch. "It's a quarter to one, which reminds me, I haven't had lunch. I'd better hurry—the director will yell if I'm late. See you around." He winked at us both and strode off. As soon as he'd left, Beth burst into giggles, and I couldn't help joining her.

"I had you pretty worried there for a minute, didn't I?" she said.

"Beth," I said, laughing, "I would've died on the spot if you'd asked him to sign that piece of paper! I would have *killed* you." I gave her a playful punch. "And it would have served you right!"

Still laughing, Beth dashed from the theater in a full sprint. Soon I was on her tail. Last fall, as sophomores at Morris High, we had both lettered in track. Beth reached the corner just ahead of me. There she slowed her pace and I took the opportunity to speed up and pass her.

As I rounded the corner, I realized why she had slowed down. Up ahead was a guy trying to push-start a beat-up blue VW bug. Beth had a soft heart for people in trouble, particularly people who were male and cute.

Together, we walked over to the car. "Having trouble?" Beth asked, a bit out of breath.

"Yeah, just a little." He grinned and wiped his brow, brushing sandy brown curls off his forehead. His eyes were green, and they sparkled.

"What's the problem?" I added.

"Well, as you can see, my car won't start." He wiped his hands on his jeans and came around to where we were standing. "Probably the battery again—either that, or she's just being stubborn."

Beth glanced at the car. "Do you live very far from here?" she asked.

"Only about five miles or so. I live on Warner Boulevard, right across from Kennedy High. I'm a junior there."

"Oh, no! We're from Morris High. It's not good for our image to be seen with our rival!" I teased.

He smiled and leaned back against his bug. "I thought I might be in enemy territory."

Beth walked to the back of the car. "I don't know if we can push you the full five miles, but we'll give you a shove and maybe that way you can at least start it."

"No, no. I couldn't ask you to do that—at least, not until I know your names." He extended his hand. "I'm Trevor Johnson."

Beth and I introduced ourselves. "This sure is a new way to meet girls," Beth said.

"Yeah, is this your usual pickup place?" I added.

Trevor gave us a wounded look. "Believe me, this is *not* a pickup—I merely need a push-start." We all laughed.

"All right," Beth said. "If you want your push, you better get ready."

"Okay, you girls are in charge." He saluted and hopped into the driver's seat as Beth and I went to the back bumper.

"Pretty cute, huh?" Beth nudged me.

"He's not bad," I admitted. "Nothing like the guy at the theater, but not bad."

"I'm ready!" Trevor hollered out the window.

We assumed our "pushing position" and went to work, but the bug only rolled ahead two or three inches, then stopped. Beth and I looked at each other and then tried again. Nothing.

"What are you carrying in that thing? Three tons of lead?" Beth called out.

"Nope." Trevor got out and joined us in back. "Maybe if we all try we can get her moving."

We all pushed and pumped and grunted for a while with no result. Wiping my sweaty forehead, I looked at Beth. Her face was all red—mine probably was, too. Putting my hands on my hips, I muttered, "This is the most stubborn car I've ever met!"

Beth nodded. "Let's give it one more try."

"Okay," Trevor agreed. "I'll move up here. Let's do it!" He opened the front door and pushed on the frame. Beth and I threw all our weight against the car and shoved and shoved. Suddenly, Trevor moaned. "The emergency brake!" he said, laughing, and reached inside. There was a "pop" and the car lurched forward. We continued to push it down the street, and the engine finally sputtered to life. Trevor promptly hopped in and drove off.

We collapsed onto the sidewalk. "What a clown!" Beth laughed and panted at the same time.

I wiped my hands on my shorts. "I can't *believe* he had the brake on the entire time!"

Trevor had flipped a U-turn, and he pulled up beside us. He leaned out the window, grinning. "Hey, you girls look tired. What on earth have you been doing?"

Beth pretended to scowl. "Pushing some bozo's car with the emergency brake on!"

He looked sheepish. "Uh, sorry about that."

"You just wanted to see us sweat," I teased.

"You girls do have a certain kind of glow," he teased back. "Listen, thanks a lot—i mean it. Let me give you a lift home."

Beth stood up. "No thanks. Actually, we were in the middle of a race when we ran into you." She looked at me and took off running.

"Gotta run," I called over my shoulder as I jumped up and raced after her.

Beth ran up the front steps of my house just a hair before me.

I tried to catch my breath. "Man, I'm pooped! I haven't been running much since track season ended."

"Me either," Beth panted. "You know, we ought to do this more often—the running, I mean, not the push-starting."

We sat on the lawn and stretched our legs. The grass felt cool against my hot skin as I lay back and closed my eyes. My heart was still pounding like crazy, and I could feel my pulse in my feet. My heart raced even faster when my thoughts turned to the theater and Jason Stuart. "You have to admit, Beth, he *is* incredible," I sighed.

"Who? The guy in the car?" she asked, massaging her leg muscles.

"Are you kidding? Jason Stuart!"

Beth smiled. "So, are we talking major crush on one seriously gorgeous guy, or what?"

"Or what. This is a potentially romantic situation." I propped myself up on my elbows and used my most dramatic voice. "At the final curtain call he sees me in the front row. He reaches down, offering me his big, strong hand. With ease he lifts me onstage. Then after one last bow, he sweeps me off my feet . . ."

Beth giggled. "You are so *corny*, Krista!"

I made a face at her. "You want to go inside for a soda or something?"

"I'd love to, but I have to go home." She stood and brushed loose grass from her legs. "I promised my mom I'd help with some gardening. I think I'll *run* home," she added, bending down in a stretch. "My thighs could use a little more thinning."

Beth was always worried about her weight, though she didn't need to at all. Track kept us in good shape, and anyway, she had a perfect figure. I watched as she took off down the street. I was definitely going to miss having her around. Pushing all thoughts of summer aside, I headed up the front steps and went inside.

Minutes later, I heard the car pulling into the driveway. My mother flung open the back door. I could see her short, curly brown hair poking over the bags of groceries she was carrying.

"Krista!" she hollered. "Would you help me with these groceries?"

"Sure," I answered, taking two of the bags. Setting them on the kitchen table, I dug through one until I found the Oreos. Mom always bought a package on Saturday, and between my little brother, Bobby, and me, they usually didn't make it past Tuesday. Taking a handful, I collapsed in a chair.

"I hope you haven't gotten into the Oreos," Mo—that's short for Mom—said as she set another load of groceries on the table.

"Now, would I do a dreadful thing like that?" I tried to keep a straight face, but I couldn't. I started cracking up, sending chocolate cookie crumbs all down my front.

She smiled and shook her head. "Be sure and clean that up."

Mo and I get along very well. As far as mothers go, I consider myself pretty lucky.

"How was your afternoon?" she asked.

I thought about Beth leaving. "Oh, it's going to be awful this summer without Beth," I said. "She's leaving as soon as school lets out."

"Oh, that's right. She's going to help out at Camp Watanda for a while."

"Not only for a while. She'll be gone most of the summer. There will be absolutely *nothing* for me to do. I'll be completely bored. In fact, I'm bored already, and it's only the middle of May!"

"Well, why don't you clean your room?" Mo suggested. "I think there's a shovel in the garage."

"Very funny." I scowled. "Seriously, Mo, what am I going to do this summer?"

She thought a minute. "Well, you could take a job."

I wrinkled my nose. "A job?"

"I read in the paper this morning that they'll be needing some help downtown at the Community Playhouse."

That grabbed my attention immediately. "What kind of help?" I asked.

Mo took a newspaper from the top of the recycling stack and began reading aloud: " 'The All-Teen Young Repertory Company will be presenting *Summer Enchantment* at the Community Playhouse in July, written and directed by David Colby and starring Trina Carlson and Jason Stuart.' He's a nice-looking boy, isn't he?" She turned the paper so I could see Jason's picture.

Nice-looking doesn't begin to describe him, I thought.

She continued, "The article goes on to say that most of the people in the play are teen-agers from this area, and they need a few more apprentices to work backstage. Why not check it out? Apprentices don't get paid, but it would certainly give you something to do while Beth's away."

Mo handed me the paper. I skipped down to the part about the job. " 'Backstage people will be needed. If you have any background in theater and are interested, contact Penny Stevenson at the Playhouse the last week in June.'

"Well, I don't have much experience, but I might give it a try," I said.

Mo nodded approvingly. "I think you'd really enjoy it."

I picked up the paper and took it to my room. Stretching out on the floor, I gazed down at Jason's picture.

"Jason Stuart," I whispered. This time I read the whole article. It listed Jason's theater credits—he'd been in at least a dozen plays and musicals at Kennedy High. *He'd* certainly had plenty of experience. Maybe I wasn't good enough even to work backstage.

I thought about it for a while, then decided there was only one way to find out. I'd call Penny Stevenson at the end of June. Since that was six weeks away, I'd have plenty of time to change my mind. But somehow, gazing at Jason's handsome face, I didn't think I would!

Chapter Two

To my surprise, the next six weeks flew by. I hadn't told Beth yet about the possibility of my working at the Playhouse because I'd been tempted several times to chicken out. But whenever I looked at the picture of Jason, which I had cut out of the paper and tucked away in my desk drawer, I knew I just had to give it a shot.

Taking a deep breath, I reached for the phone by my bed and dialed the number of the theater. I couldn't believe I was actually doing it!

When a woman answered, I said, "Uh . . . may I speak with Penny Stevenson?"

"This is Penny," the woman replied.

Trying to hide my nervousness, I said, "Hi! My name is Krista Winters. I read in the paper a while ago that you were looking for stagehands."

"That's right. Are you interested?"

"Yes, I am." I knew what she'd ask next, and she did.

"So, Krista, do you have any background in musical theater?"

"Well, I played the Scarecrow in *The Wizard of Oz* in fifth grade. I've seen a lot of shows at the Playhouse, and I sometimes sing in the shower." I turned beet-red, realizing how idiotic I must have sounded.

Penny laughed. "That's fine," she said. "Most of last year's crew have come back for this season, but we still have room for one more. Why don't you come down to the Playhouse next Saturday morning at ten? I can learn more about you, and you can take a look around."

"Okay—thanks! I'll be there!" I babbled, amazed that she hadn't hung up on me after the shower bit.

I ran over to my desk and took out the picture of Jason. "See you on Saturday, maybe," I told the photograph.

"Krista, would you please turn that alarm off!"

I rolled over and saw my mother in the doorway with her hands on her hips. Then the nagging beeps of my alarm clock finally registered.

"Nine-thirty!" I yelped and bounded out of bed, nearly running over Mo in my mad dash for the shower. "I'm going to be soooo late!"

"So late for what?" she asked. "You haven't been up this early since school let out."

"The job!" I hollered over the running water. "I told you I got the job at the theater, remember? I'm supposed to be there at ten!"

"I'll fix breakfast, then."

Once I had finished my shower, I couldn't decide what to put on. What did stagehands wear, anyway? I pawed through my closet and threw everything onto my bed.

Mo entered my room with a toasted bagel on a plate. "Your blue sundress," she said.

"But I'm supposed to be a stagehand."

"You look good in your blue sundress." She set the plate down and left.

"Mothers," I mumbled, but I took her advice. As soon as I was dressed, I grabbed the bagel and ran outside to my truck. I climbed in, and started the monster. If only my mother wasn't so paranoid about me driving a small car! This pickup was much more difficult to handle than a nice little compact.

I pulled into the theater parking lot two minutes behind schedule. "Well, ready or not, here I come," I muttered to myself as I smoothed the skirt of my blue sundress. Then I got out of the truck and hurried to the back door of the theater.

It was very dark inside compared to the bright sunshine. At first I felt blinded.

"Krista Winters?" someone asked from somewhere in the darkness.

"Yes, that's me," I called in the direction of the voice. When my eyes adjusted to the dim light, I saw a short girl about my age coming toward me. She had on jeans and a bright red shirt.

"Hi! I'm Carol, part of the stage crew. Penny—she's the stage manager—is in the greenroom with the rest of the crew. She sent me out here to wait for you. You're late, you know." She talked very fast and all in one breath.

"Yes, I know. I'm really sorry. I woke up a little late this morning," I told her.

I followed Carol through several doors and down several hallways. We finally arrived at a door marked Greenroom. When we went inside, it wasn't green. I wondered why it was called that, but I didn't ask.

Penny was sitting on a wooden stool in the center of the room. Five teenagers were gathered around her, seated on various pieces of furniture and props.

"Krista? I'm Penny Stevenson." The tall, slender woman stood and extended a hand to me. Her long, dark hair was tied back with a colorful scarf, and her smile was friendly. "I'm the stage manager. I do the hiring—and

16

firing—of stagehands." She looked over at a guy seated on a counter. "Remember that, Trevor," she said with a grin.

Trevor grinned at me and winked. My mouth dropped open. He was the guy in the VW bug that Beth and I had pushed, over a month ago!

Turning back to me, Penny continued, "This is the shift crew. They take care of props, costumes, and scenery changes. I have a separate tech crew for lighting and sound. Being a stagehand isn't too complicated. Think you can handle it?"

"Yeah . . . sure," I said, not so sure that I meant it.

"Great! You start tomorrow. We work nine to four with an hour for lunch. Hey, Trevor," Penny said, "show Krista around—give her the grand tour."

"Yes, ma'am!" He jumped off the counter, and I noticed that he was almost a head taller than I. I liked the way his sandy brown hair curled in the back.

"This is our lovely greenroom," he said with a grand gesture, "where our *beloved* actors and dancers assemble before they trip the light fantastic."

Penny rolled her eyes. "*Trevor.* Knock it off. Why don't you start with props and costumes?"

He did an about-face. "Follow me," he said to me over his shoulder.

As we went out of the room, he said, "I didn't expect to see you here. Is this your first stage job?"

"Uh . . . yeah. What gave it away?" I hadn't said anything stupid yet, had I?

"I think it was the dress. Don't get me wrong—it's a very nice dress, but we usually don't wear dresses backstage." He grinned. "In fact, I *never* wear dresses."

I laughed. "Actually, it was my mother's suggestion."

"Your mother dresses you?" he teased.

"Only on special occasions," I said, laughing. I noted what he was wearing. "I guess jeans and T-shirts are more appropriate?"

Trevor nodded. "You got it. But I really like that dress."

We headed down a flight of stairs that led to the basement level.

"So, how long have you been involved in the theater?" I asked him.

"I'm in the drama program at Kennedy, and I've been working here for the past two summers. The job doesn't pay, but the experience is great. Last year, I was backstage for *Grease*, and then I had an acting part in the musical *Guys and Dolls*."

"Do you want to be an actor or a stagehand?" I asked.

"Neither." He grinned. "I want to be a director, but to do that, you have to know all about acting and technical support."

We reached the bottom floor where there was a whole underground network of light blue hallways with royal blue doors. It looked like an easy place to get lost.

Trevor flung open a door. "This is the prop room."

It was huge. Inside were rows and rows of shelves filled with all kinds of odds and ends, everything from desk lamps and telephones to grandfather clocks and statues. Larger items that were too big to fit on the shelves were lined up in rows along one side of the room.

"Where did they get all this stuff?" I wondered aloud.

"Probably went to a lot of garage sales." Trevor picked up a golf club and took a couple of practice swings. "You name it, we got it."

"A kaleidoscope," I said impulsively.

He scratched his head. "North wall, third row, fifth shelf down on the right side."

I gave him a skeptical look, then followed his directions. Sure enough, there was a kaleidoscope.

"Alphabetical order," he said smugly. "This is the *K* section. Each theater basically does it their own way. Here it's A through Z. Well, enough show-and-tell. We have another room to explore."

The costume room down the hall was as big as the prop room, and filled with racks and racks of clothes. Some were even suspended from the ceiling.

"We raise and lower them with pulleys," Trevor said, as if he were reading my mind. He walked over to one of the racks. "The costumes in this room are grouped by time period." He picked a feathered hat off a rack and tossed it to me. "My favorites are from the early seventeenth century." Trevor grabbed a purple cloak off another rack. "Sometimes I think I was born in the wrong era." He jumped up on a table, pulled the cloak around him, then rattled off several phrases I recognized from Shakespearean plays I had read in English class.

He hopped down and asked, "Have you ever done any acting?"

"Well, I played the Scarecrow in *The Wizard of Oz* in fifth grade," I admitted.

"That's a start," he said, taking the hat from me. "Wait a minute! Are you the one who sings in the shower?"

I felt my face turn flaming red. Penny must have mentioned my phone call! I wondered if everyone in the whole theater knew. Maybe even Jason had heard.

"Hey, I think it's great," Trevor said, before I could panic. "C'mon—it's about time to head on up."

He locked the door, and we started back up to ground level. Trevor led the way down a hall and opened a door. I immediately heard singing, and guessed that we were back-stage. It was so dark that I couldn't see two steps in front of me.

"Careful, there's a lot of junk back here," he warned.

I stuck my hands out in front of me, grop-ing around. "Ouch!" I hit something with my foot. Next I bumped my leg, and then I nearly strangled myself on some ropes that hung down from the ceiling. At last, I could see light from the stage.

"Attention, everyone! Attention!" Trevor shouted as he stepped out from the wings, clapping his hands loudly.

"What's going on?" A large, round, bald man looked up from a script he was marking. "Oh, it's you, Trevor." He sighed. "I should have known!"

Trevor dragged me out to center stage. "I want to introduce you all to the newest mem-ber of our crew, Krista Winters."

I could feel everyone in the cast staring at me. I was so embarrassed, I wished I could sink through the floor.

The bald man shook my hand. "Nice to meet you, Krista. I'm David Colby, director of this shinding."

"It's my pleasure," I said weakly.

"This is Trina Carlson, our leading lady." Mr. Colby motioned to a tall, attractive girl with wavy brown hair and dark eyes. She nodded. "And our leading man, Jason Stuart."

Jason walked over and took my hand. "Nice to meet you, Krista," he said, giving it a squeeze before he released it.

I had dreamed about this moment so many times! I tried to say something, but nothing came out, so I just nodded.

"Does this mean we're taking a break? Shall we have a little get-acquainted party?" A cool voice brought me abruptly back to reality, and I saw Trina scowling.

"We're outta here!" Trevor threw a kiss to Trina, and grabbed my hand, dragging me offstage. "Exit, stage left!"

Once we were backstage, he said, "Don't mind Trina. She's a real prima donna. I've had to put up with her for two years in drama at Kennedy—she drives me crazy. But she gets all the lead roles in our musicals. Boy, can she sing!"

We walked through the obstacle course again, but this time I managed to steer clear of everything.

"Well, this is our happy home. Any questions?" Trevor asked when we came into the lobby, his eyes twinkling.

This guy was a bundle of energy! I wondered if there was an "off" switch. I smiled. "No, not yet."

"You've had the grand tour, so you can

take off if you want. Like Penny said, we start working nine o'clock tomorrow."

I nodded. "Okay. I think I'll just look around a little more, if that's okay?"

"Sure, no problem. If any questions pop up, I'll be in the greenroom, or the prop room, or the scene shop," Trevor said as he hurried off.

Quietly opening the door to the theater, I slipped into a seat in the back row. Jason and Trina were onstage with the chorus. Looking over the crowd, I recognized a couple of kids from my school, including Marcie Lopez. She'd always had a bad attitude in algebra—maybe she'd be nicer at the theater.

Mr. Colby was addressing the cast as he paced the front of the stage. "This is a *happy* scene. I want to see happy faces on everyone. You look as though you're going to a funeral. Let's get happy!" He clapped his hands. "Again from the top." A few groans were quickly squelched by his sharp glance. The cast scrambled back to their places as Mr. Colby cued the piano player.

The song began with Trina singing a solo. Trevor was right—she did have a gorgeous voice. Then Jason joined in, his deep, powerful baritone blending with her sweet soprano. Soon the full chorus took over and the stage came alive with singing and dancing. Oh, how I loved musicals!

When the number ended, Mr. Colby applauded. "Okay—better. Much better! Let's break for lunch. One hour, everybody. Be back here by one o'clock!"

I stayed in my seat, listening to the chatter as the cast broke up into groups and left the stage. Jason stayed behind, talking to Mr. Colby. I watched as he pointed to his script, listened to what the director had to say, and nodded. Then, hopping off the stage, he came jogging up the center aisle. Maybe he was going to talk to me! I got all nervous and my hands started sweating.

"Jason!" I blurted out before I could stop myself.

He stopped next to my seat and smiled. "Oh, hi, Krista. Nice to have you aboard. I think you'll enjoy working on the show." Then he looked at me again, more closely this time. "You know, you look kinda familiar . . ." He shook his head, then glanced at his watch. "Gotta run." He smiled and left.

I couldn't believe I'd talked to him. We'd made contact the very first day! I could hardly wait to tell Beth all about it.

I felt like skipping out to my truck, but I managed to walk normally. Still, I was smiling so hard that my cheeks started to ache.

The first thing I did when I got home was call Beth. "I was onstage with him," I squealed into the phone. "I *spoke* to him, and he knew my name, and he *recognized* me!"

"Who are you talking about? Where have you been? I have been roasting myself for over an hour, waiting for you to show up." Beth sounded a little cross.

Suddenly I remembered that we had planned to spend her last day before she left for camp tanning by her pool. "Beth, I'm so sorry. I'll be over in two minutes!"

I grabbed my swimsuit and dashed out the door. There was so much to tell her about my first day at the theater. And wait till she heard that I had actually held hands with Jason Stuart—well, almost.

Chapter Three

"So you really have a job at the Playhouse?" Beth sat up and peered at me through her sunglasses as we lounged by her pool. "You never cease to amaze me, Krista."

I told her about meeting Trevor again, and his grand tour of the theater. Then I skipped to the exciting part. "Jason Stuart came right up to me after rehearsal and said, 'Welcome aboard, Krista.' "

"He actually came over and *talked* to you?"

"Well, the director introduced us. But he *did* say hello, and he *does* know my name."

"Did he remember you?" Beth asked.

"I'm not sure. But he did say I looked familiar." I sighed. "And he's even more gorgeous than he looks in his picture."

Beth lay back down on her towel and

closed her eyes. "Tell me more about Trevor," she mumbled.

"Trevor!" I wrinkled my nose. "He's a total spaz!"

Beth giggled. "Sounds perfect for you!"

"Get real," I snapped. "I'm not interested in Trevor. He's a lot of fun, but he's definitely not my type."

"Oh, I forgot. Jason is your one true love," Beth said dramatically.

I threw my bottle of sunscreen at her.

Beth yelped, and then she started to scream. A small, fuzzy bee was crawling along the edge of her towel.

"Krista!" she shrieked. "Get it away!" Beth was petrified. There's nothing she hates more than bees. I didn't see what the big deal was, but then again, I'd never been stung. I shooed the creature away, and Beth acted as if I'd saved her life.

We swam in her pool a couple of times, and finally Beth looked at her watch. "I guess we'd better go inside," she said. "I don't have much time left. Camp Watanda awaits."

In Beth's room, I sat on her bed while she quickly showered and changed, then finished packing for her trip.

"Promise you'll keep me posted on what's going on at the theater," she said, stuffing a couple extra pairs of socks into one of her two duffel bags.

"You know I will." I carefully folded the slip of paper she had given me with her address on it. "And if you don't write to me at least once a week, don't bother to come home," I teased.

We heard the front door open. "Beth!" her father called. "Time to go!"

"Well, it looks like I'm out of here." She picked up one bag, I grabbed the other, and we took them out and tossed them in the trunk of her dad's car.

"Have fun with the camp kids," I said, feeling suddenly sad.

"*You* have fun with the theater boys," Beth said, and got into the front seat next to her father.

I waved wildly until the car turned the corner. Boy, was I going to miss my best friend! At least I had the theater to keep me busy.

It was close to six now, so I raced home. I was pushing it—my dad is an eat-at-six kind of guy.

When I came in, the table was set, and my parents and my five-year-old brother were already seated. Even the salad was served. I slipped into the empty chair.

"So how's the latest member of the work force?" Dad asked as he spooned a helping of peas onto his plate.

"Yes, dear, how did it go?" Mo added. "Did you meet that good-looking boy?"

"It was fine," I replied, avoiding the *boy* issue.

Dad smiled at me. "That's great. You know, I remember my first job. I was about your age, and . . ."

I had set him rolling. All through dinner he and my mother reminisced about their past work experiences, so I let them chatter while I concentrated on my chicken to avoid looking at Bobby. He was putting peas in his mouth one at a time and then spitting them back on his plate when he thought our parents weren't watching. Little brothers are so gross!

My mind wandered to the theater and Jason's words to me. "Hi, Krista. Nice to have you aboard." I heard him say it over and over again. I could see his deep blue eyes looking down at me. Perhaps he was thinking about me right now, wondering where he had seen me before. I kind of hoped he wouldn't remember.

The next morning, I put on my second-best jeans and a bright yellow T-shirt. I found the other stagehands in the greenroom, and took a seat on an old tweed sofa. Carol was chatting with a short guy with glasses who was dressed all in black. A tall, thin boy leaned against the wall, reading a magazine. Across the room, in front of the long counter where

Trevor had sat yesterday, were two more boys. They were facing away from me, but I could see them in the long mirror behind them. They looked like identical twins.

"The gang's all here," Trevor said, as he burst into the room, followed by Penny.

"We've got a lot of work to do today," Penny said briskly. She grabbed an empty chair, and everyone gathered around. "The show opens next week, so from today until Sunday we'll have run-throughs with scene changes. Then beginning Monday it will be dress and tech rehearsals." She opened her book of notes. "Colby is working with the cast outside this morning, so they'll be out of our hair for a while. He gave me a list of extra props he needs. Carol, why don't you and the twins run down and get them from the prop room."

Carol took the sheet of paper Penny handed her. "Right. We'll put them backstage." She motioned to the twins, and the three of them left.

"Trevor . . ." Penny checked her notes again. "The curtains on stage right need to be adjusted. You take Alan and Rodney." The guy with glasses and the thin boy with the magazine followed Trevor out the door.

Now I was the only one left. I sat waiting for my task as Penny flipped through several pages. She seemed to have forgotten all about me.

"Uh—what about me?" I finally asked, feeling awkward.

"Oh, Krista! I'm sorry—there's so much to do with the show opening next week that I don't know which end is up." She ran her hands through her hair, which she'd worn loose today. "I have some boxes of equipment in my car. You can come and help me bring them in."

I hurried after her to the parking lot. Next to the lot was a little park with a stream running through it. The cast members were going over a scene while Mr. Colby paced back and forth, watching intently and making occasional comments.

After a moment I spotted Jason. He was wearing a royal blue cutoff sweatshirt with the sleeves pushed up to reveal strong, muscular arms. I wished I could hide behind a tree and watch him all morning. At the moment he was chasing a pretty blond girl from the chorus around in circles. I wished I could have been in her place, only I would have let him catch me!

"Here you go." Penny handed me a box of electrical cables that she had taken from the trunk of her car. Reluctantly, I tore myself away from the park and headed back to the theater.

A short while later, all the crew gathered onstage while Penny went through each scene, explaining how each set change was supposed to work, and what we'd each be responsible for.

After we had put the garden set in place, she said, "Okay, now we switch to inside the house. Krista, you and Alan take off the trellis and bring in the china cabinet. . . ."

I looked over at the cabinet, which was very large, and then at Alan, who was shorter than I was. "Excuse me. Isn't that a little heavy for just the two of us?" I asked.

Trevor answered for Penny. "I think you can manage it. All the big, heavy stuff is on rollers—you just wheel it out and lock it down."

We continued going through each change. Penny explained how parts of the sets revolved, and others lowered from the ceiling which she called "the flies." I was responsible mainly for bringing props on and off stage.

Carol stuck her head around the curtain and said, "I put the extra flowers on the prop cart."

"Thanks," I whispered. That was supposed to be my job, but I'd forgotten about it.

"How do you remember where everything goes?" I asked Trevor at one point.

He grabbed an umbrella off a table. "You just picture the set in your mind." He closed his eyes. "And then you ask yourself, 'If I were an umbrella, where would I be?'" He opened his eyes and grinned. "Don't worry—you'll get the hang of it. And if you forget, Penny will post a flow sheet backstage. It lists every cue in the entire show."

I sure hoped so. There was so much to remember.

"Everything has to be perfect. This play is really important to Mr. Colby. He wrote it himself, you know," Trevor told me. "This is the first time it's ever been performed."

"I've seen bits and pieces. What's it about?" I asked.

"It's a love story, set in the Midwest. The girl, Trina, lives on a farm and the guy, Jason, is from the big city. They fall in love, of course, and her parents don't approve. So they have to disguise themselves and meet secretly in the barn, the garden, the train station, the Soda Shoppe. . . ."

Before he could tell me more, Penny yelled, "Okay! Ready for the final scene!"

Trevor dashed off and everyone else scurried to take their positions. I ran through my list of responsibilities in my head: First, help Rodney strike the desk from the previous scene, then bring out the park bench and the trash can and finally, arrange the fake flowers.

For the rest of the morning as we rehearsed the changes over and over, I started to get a feel for what went where. But by lunchtime I was exhausted.

I went back to the greenroom and plopped down on the sofa, putting my aching feet on the coffee table. It was pretty scuffed—maybe this was a typical stagehand resting spot. I closed my eyes.

Trevor woke me from my two-second nap. "Hey, the twins and I are getting some lunch. Wanna come?"

I was hungry, but not hungry enough to move. "I don't think I can—my body's on strike," I told him.

"Then we'll bring you a burger." A moment later he was gone.

I didn't even hear the door close. I was in dreamland, running through a wide open field filled with wildflowers, and Jason was chasing me. He caught up to me and put an arm around my waist. We stood gazing into each other's eyes. Then we were running through the fields again hand in hand, in slow motion. . . .

"Here you go, Sleeping Beauty!" I was jerked awake when a McDonald's bag landed in my lap. Trevor stood in the doorway. "You have exactly five minutes to eat and get backstage."

I was glad he left—I didn't want anyone to see the way I gobbled up that burger and fries. I was absolutely starved—maybe it was from running through the fields.

I joined the others backstage with only seconds to spare. I could hear the cast assembling onstage, and my heart skipped. I'd see Jason all afternoon!

"We'll be doing complete run-throughs for the rest of the day," Penny told us, "so the scene changes will come as they do in the show. Watch for your cues."

Peeking through the curtains, I saw Jason talking to Trina. His dark hair was tousled from the breeze outside, and he looked super.

A few minutes later the run-through began, and we went through the show scene by scene.

"How's it going, sport?" Trevor whispered from behind me as I grabbed two sundae dishes and two fountain stools.

"Pretty good. I'm catching on pretty quick."

Trevor shook his head and smiled. "I don't think they serve ice cream in the church scene. The Soda Shoppe is the scene after next."

I gasped and ran to switch props. I had to make sure to use my head. It would be so embarrassing to make a mistake in front of Jason.

About halfway through, Trevor came over to the side of the stage where I was standing.

"I have to go to the dentist," he whispered. "I'll be gone the rest of the day. Think you can possibly survive without me?"

"I might be able to make it—if I can remember about no ice cream in church!" I said with a giggle.

"Good. Now how about a jump-start?" he asked.

I stared at him. "What?"

"My car—it needs a jump-start. I think it's the battery—it's been acting up lately, so I keep a set of jumper cables handy. It'll only take a minute." He waved toward the stage. "They just started the scene. They won't miss you."

We hurried out to the parking lot. "My pride and joy," Trevor said, patting the hood of the beat-up bug. He popped open the hood, and took out the jumper cables. I pulled my truck next to his car, and we hooked up the cables. After a few revs of my engine, the VW began sputtering and back-firing. I could hear it cough its way down the street as I ran back into the theater.

"Where are the briefcase and the desk lamp for this scene?" I heard Mr. Colby yelling as I slipped in through the stage door.

"Oh, no!" I groaned. I had missed my cue. Now I had to run out in front of everyone with the props they needed.

And that was just the beginning. Things went from bad to worse. First I forgot the dishes, then I hung the pictures upside down. Next I put the hats and canes stage left instead of stage right. I kept checking Penny's flow sheet, but I still couldn't seem to get anything right.

Finally we reached the next-to-last scene of

37

the second act. Only two more and I could go home. The setting was a railway station, so I wheeled out a huge trunk, and hurried to grab my other props.

I had just scooted offstage when the scene opened with Jason and several chorus members doing a big dance number. Jason leapt up on top of the trunk—and it began to roll.

"Oh, no!" I moaned. I had left the dolly under the trunk!

Unable to keep his balance, Jason flailed his arms wildly. As I watched in horror, he toppled over backward.

"What idiot forgot to remove the wheels?" he yelled, getting to his feet. Thank goodness he wasn't hurt!

Mr. Colby strode over to the trunk and pulled the dolly out from underneath. *"Penny!"* he bellowed. "Tell your crew to get their act together! I don't want anything like this to happen again!"

I forced myself to walk out onstage, though I desperately wanted to hide behind the side curtains and let someone else take the blame. "Excuse me, sir," I said to Mr. Colby. "It's my fault. I'm the one who forgot to remove the dolly. I'm terribly sorry."

"You are *so* stupid!" Trina shrieked at me. "I don't want you ever handling any of *my* props! Jason could have broken his neck!" She glared at me and called over her shoulder as she stomped offstage, "You really don't belong here!"

Mr. Colby waited until she had left, then looked at me. "It's all right, Krista. But please be more careful next time." He turned and addressed the cast. "Okay, gang, let's call it a day."

I looked over at Jason, but he was surrounded by some of the chorus dancers. If only I could talk to him, let him know how awful I felt about the trunk! The whole day had been a disaster. Obviously Trina was right—I didn't belong in the theater. They needed someone with experience for this type of stuff. I'd just ruin everything.

Silent and miserable, I left the stage. I was definitely going to quit this job. Maybe I could get hired at the Market Basket bagging groceries.

I stopped by the greenroom to pick up my purse. But instead of heading for the parking lot, I went around to the front of the building.

This is what started it all, I thought, walking over to the glass case and gazing at Jason's photograph. I must have been crazy to think I could do a good job in the theater.

"What's the matter? Don't you like my picture?" Jason's voice startled me.

"Oh, no! I love it! I mean, it's a really good picture. Oh, Jason, I'm so sorry about . . ."

"Hey, these things happen." He smiled at me, and I suddenly felt weak in the knees. His broad shoulders blocked out the sun so I could look right into his beautiful blue eyes without squinting.

"People get really stressed out before the opening of a show," he went on, "so don't worry about it. I think you did pretty well, considering it's your first day."

I grimaced. "Except for the wheels."

"Except for the wheels." His smile broadened, and I found myself smiling back.

"I have to get going, but I'll see you tomorrow, Krista." He turned and started walking down the street.

"Yeah—see you tomorrow, Jason!" I called after him. I guessed I wasn't quitting after all.

Chapter Four

Rehearsals went pretty smoothly for the rest of the week. Trevor caught me twice before I fouled up scene changes, but Trina was constantly on my back about anything and everything.

Almost before I knew it, it was the day of the dress rehearsal—the show would open the following night. There was lots of excitement and tension both on stage and off. We had only two run-throughs left, one before lunch without costumes, and one after with costumes and makeup. The first rehearsal started out great, except that one of the dancers in the first act missed her cue. All the scene changes went like clockwork, making us stagehands look like pros.

But in the fourth scene of the second act,

Trina was supposed to have a mirror set out for her and it wasn't there. I didn't know who was responsible, but it wasn't me. Anyway, I grabbed it from the prop table and rushed it out to her.

The minute the scene was over, Trina stormed backstage. "Krista! If you can't put my props out right, then get someone who can!" She glared at me. "I will *not* look like a fool because of your incompetence."

Trevor came up behind her. "Look, Trina, why don't you get off her case? Krista has nothing to do with the mirror. If you want to yell at someone, then yell at me. But you know I won't be listening."

Trina tossed her head and flounced away.

"Keep it up, Trina," Trevor called after her, "and you just might be missing a prop or two on opening night!"

She didn't say a word, and just kept on walking.

Trevor turned to me and shrugged. "Sometimes the only way to deal with our prima donna is to throw some of her nastiness back in her face." He smiled and crossed over behind the set to his side of the stage.

I thought it was so cool of Trevor to stand up for me. He was turning out to be a terrific friend.

I felt a tap on my shoulder and turned around. "Thanks, Krista," Alan whispered. "I completely forgot about Trina's mirror."

"No problem," I whispered back.

The finale went on without problems. "Okay! Cast and crew onstage!" Mr. Colby hollered.

Shielding my eyes from the glare of the stage lights as I came out of the wings, I wondered how the actors and actresses were able to find their way around with all those lights constantly shining in their eyes.

"Tomorrow is the real thing—opening night!" Mr. Colby said when we were all together. "But there's still a lot to do. So let's take a quick lunch and be back in plenty of time to get into your makeup and costumes."

As everybody chattered and moved off the stage, Trevor came up next to me.

"Krista, how about a hand with a push-start in a couple minutes?" He waited only long enough for a nod from me and then hurried to catch up with Mr. Colby. "Hey, Mr. Colby, that last scene looks great," I heard him say sincerely. "There's a lot of emotion in it. It's a strong ending—it really works for me."

"Thanks, Trevor," Mr. Colby said as they walked out the side door.

I was the only one left backstage. Everyone else had already gone for lunch—except Jason.

He was sitting on the edge of the stage, changing from his dancing shoes into sneakers, and I decided to say something to him. Feeling terribly self-conscious, I walked out onto the stage. Butterflies were spinning in my stomach, and I felt as though a spotlight were following my every move. Not quite sure how to begin, I remembered what Trevor had just said.

"The last scene looks great," I told Jason.

He looked up and smiled. "Oh, hi, Krista." He laced his other shoe. "You really like the finale?"

"Yeah. There's a lot of emotion in it. It's a strong ending." I felt a little guilty parroting Trevor's exact words, but they had sounded so perfect.

Jason looked uncertain. "Really? I kind of feel like I've been forcing it."

"Oh, no—it really works for me," I assured him.

"That's terrific." Jason stood up and brushed off the seat of his pants. "It's a workout, that's for sure. I'm starved. Got any plans for lunch?"

I shook my head. "Not really."

"Well then, let's go grab something before the one o'clock call. How about Henry's? They make an incredible sub sandwich."

"Sounds great!" I said happily. Then I remembered that I had told Trevor I'd help him start his car. He would probably kill me later, but I couldn't pass up this opportunity.

We walked together toward the parking lot. I couldn't believe I was going out to lunch with Jason Stuart! I would have to write Beth at camp and tell her all about this.

Jason unlocked the door of his beautiful blue Camaro and we got in. He had just started to pull out of the lot when he looked in the rearview mirror, stopped the car, and started laughing. I stuck my head out the window and looked behind us.

There was Trevor, trying to push-start his VW by himself! He'd give it a shove to get it rolling, then hop inside and try to start it.

"Just a minute," Jason said. He got out of the car and went over to give Trevor a hand, but they couldn't seem to get the VW started. Then to my horror, Jason brought Trevor back with him. Our romantic lunch date was ruined!

"Hey, Krista," Trevor said, climbing into the backseat. "I was looking for you."

Jason slid behind the wheel. "We're heading over to Henry's," he said over his shoulder.

"Cool! They make an incredible meatball sandwich," Trevor said.

"Nah. Their sub's much better," Jason insisted. The two of them argued good-naturedly about their favorite sandwiches all the way over to the restaurant while I sat there and fumed.

At Henry's we found a booth and ordered our sandwiches. I was still mad. Jason and I could have been alone together. Instead, the two guys talked nonstop while I just sat there silently and ate my sub.

They stopped talking long enough for Trevor to comment, "You're sure quiet, Krista." They were both staring at me, waiting for me to answer. I didn't know it was a question.

"Just enjoying my lunch," I said with a shrug. Then the two of them were at it again, this time comparing notes on Kennedy High's sports statistics. Trevor had played soccer for three years, while Jason had divided his time between baseball and the theater. I guess I could have joined in the conversation, quoting my track stats, but I wasn't in the mood.

On the way back to the theater, I sat in the backseat.

"I'm going to drop you two off," Jason said, pulling up in front of the theater. "I have to get something I said I'd pick up for Colby. There's no sense in us all being late."

Actually, I wouldn't have minded being late if I had had a chance to talk with him. I was about to suggest that I ride along on Jason's errand when Trevor hopped out and opened the door for me. Reluctantly, I got out, too.

"Aren't you glad you stuck with the sub instead of the meatball sandwich?" Jason asked, winking at me.

I couldn't help but smile. He was so good looking. "You were right, it was super. See you inside," I said, carefully closing the car door.

"I don't know. I still think the meatball sandwich is unbeatable," Trevor insisted as we walked into the lobby.

I didn't say anything. I was really annoyed with him for butting in on my lunch date.

Throughout the afternoon rehearsal, I avoided Trevor. I just didn't feel like talking to him. How could I explain to him what I was thinking—or feeling?

At the end of the dress rehearsal, Penny gathered the crew in the greenroom. "Okay. Tomorrow is the big night. I think we have everything under control, though we need to speed up the change between the fourth and fifth scenes of act two. Remember, it's our job to help make these people look terrific." She paged through some notes. "The call is six o'clock tomorrow night. I know that's early for an eight o'clock curtain, but I want us to be absolutely ready. Normally you can get here at seven, and your days will be free except on Wednesdays and Saturdays when we do matinees. Remember, I want you dressed all in black, including socks and shoes, like Alan." Alan, who always wore black, lifted up his pant legs.

She continued, "That's so you'll be virtually invisible when you make scene changes during the blackouts. All right, that's it. I'll see you here tomorrow, six o'clock sharp!" She headed for the door, and the stagehands quickly grabbed their stuff. It had been a long day.

"What's up with you, Krista?" Trevor asked as I was about to leave. "You haven't said a single word to me since lunch." He waited for me to respond. When I didn't, he asked, "What did I do? Did I say something wrong?"

"I'm sorry. I'm just a little tired." I knew he didn't buy my excuse, but I couldn't tell him I was head over heels for Jason Stuart.

"So are we still friends?" Trevor gave me a puppy-dog look. I nodded. It was sure hard to stay mad with him always joking around. Trevor grinned. "Terrific. Now how about helping me with jumper cables, friend?"

I laughed, and followed Trevor out to the parking lot.

Opening night was a huge success! The applause from the audience roared on and on, and the cast took six curtain calls. If they took any more, I thought Rodney's arms would fall off from opening and closing the curtains. Everything had gone perfectly. Every prop was in its place, every song was right on key, and every dancer was in step.

Right after the show, I looked for Jason to congratulate him on his performance. I thought he had been even more brilliant than usual. Perhaps he would take my hand and squeeze it, like he had when we first met. Even thinking about it sent a little shiver through me. But I was too late—he had fled to his dressing room to take off his costume and makeup.

"Krista!" I heard Trina calling me. "I need my cape pressed for tomorrow night. Make sure it's done." She tossed the wrinkled garment at me as she left the stage. I couldn't figure out why she was always so rotten to me—I certainly hadn't done anything to her.

"Krista, hurry up!" This time it was Carol calling me. We were the last of the crew onstage.

"I'm coming!" I yelled. "I have to get my purse."

"Could you turn out the lights and close the door after you? I really gotta run."

I heard her close the door as I found my purse buried under a bunch of other things on the prop table. Then I found the backstage light switch on the other side of the stage and turned off the overhead lights. The stage went black except for the faint glow cast by one work light on a stand. I had to wait a minute or two until my eyes got used to the dimness.

It was so quiet with everyone gone that I could hear my sneakers squeak as I walked across the stage. In the middle, I paused, looking out at the hundreds of shadowy seats in the empty house.

"Hello!" I said. My voice sounded very loud in the stillness. Feeling kind of silly, I laughed. Then for some stupid reason, I started saying some of Trina's lines. I was surprised at how many of her speeches I knew by heart.

"Oh, Bernard! The flowers are lovely! . . ." I began. I went through the first scene, acting the part of the girl Jason, who played Bernard, loved. When the time came for Trina's solo, I stood center stage and sang to the empty seats.

"Love makes everything beautiful . . ." Oh, wow! I sure sounded terrible! I decided I'd better stick to singing in the shower.

Wandering over to the apron of the stage, I peered into the orchestra pit. It was a long way down—I would hate to fall down there, especially with no one around. I got up and ran to center stage.

"Look at me, everybody! I'm Trina Carlson," I shouted, imitating her voice. "I'm a star, and I'm *terrific*!" I tossed my head and strutted around the stage.

"Hey, Trina!" a deep voice called, and I froze.

Somebody had come onstage.

"Trina?"

This time I recognized the voice. It was Jason! He must have heard me fooling around. I felt like an idiot. What was I going to do? I couldn't just run and hide. Where was he, anyway?

"Uh, hi, Krista." I must have jumped ten feet. He was right behind me. "I thought you were . . ."

". . . Trina," I finished for him. I could barely make out Jason's features, but I could see his smile even in the dim light.

"What are you still doing here?" he asked, obviously amused.

"I—I . . ." I couldn't think of any reason why I was strutting around on an empty stage, singing my lungs out to an empty house.

Before I could say any more, Jason said, "Well, I'm glad you are here. I have a flat tire. I've been trying to get the car up, but my jack wouldn't hold. You wouldn't happen to have a jack in that truck of yours, by any chance?"

I grinned. "Today is your lucky day. I just happen to have a great jack under my front seat."

"Super!" He took my hand and started for the backstage door. "Come on—I know my way out of here with my eyes closed."

He was holding my hand! I couldn't believe I was actually holding hands with Jason Stuart. His hand was so warm, and so strong. I bet his arms would feel wonderful around me. The thought of being in Jason's arms made my head spin. When we got outside I felt really dizzy. I stumbled, and he put his arm around me. "Krista, are you all right?"

"I'm fine," I said breathlessly.

"You had me worried there for a minute," Jason said, releasing me. He locked the theater door, and we headed over to the moonlit parking lot.

His Camaro was parked not far from my truck. I paused in front of it, wishing I had a car like his. I was suddenly embarrassed by my pickup.

But Jason said, "This is hot. I love trucks—I wanted one, but my parents gave me the Camaro for my graduation, so I guess I can't complain."

"The only reason I drive this is because my folks couldn't find a nice, safe Brink's armored car for me," I joked, and we both laughed.

I pulled the jack out from under my front seat, thinking that what with Trevor's bug on the fritz, and now Jason's flat tire, I was turning into an all-around auto mechanic.

Handing the jack to Jason, I watched as he put it in place. I helped him loosen the lug nuts on the wheel and then he jacked up the car.

After about twenty minutes adjusting and readjusting the spare tire, Jason gave up. "It won't fit. I don't know what's wrong with the thing—it's brand-new." He wiped his hands on his jeans. "I hate to ask you, Krista, but can you give me a lift home? I don't live too far from here."

"No problem!" I hoped I didn't sound too eager.

Locking his car, he returned my jack to its place under the front seat and climbed into my truck with me. He rolled down the window, and the air ruffled his hair as I drove. I kept sneaking side glances at him, noticing how handsome he looked.

We didn't say much on the ride to his house. Aside from giving me directions, Jason was pretty quiet. He was probably thinking about his car, I figured. I'd be pretty bummed, too, if my beautiful new car had a problem.

Jason lived about two miles from the theater, in a big white two-story house, with a huge oak tree in the front yard.

"Thanks, Krista," he said as I stopped in front of it. "I really owe you one, but I promise I'll pay you back. How about another sub sandwich?"

"How about pizza?" I countered, smiling.

He smiled, too. "Pizza sounds great. I really appreciate your help. See you at the theater tomorrow." He reached out and touched my cheek, then turned and started up the front walk.

I left both windows down as I drove home. What a wonderful night! I could hardly wait to fall into bed and spend the rest of it dreaming about Jason.

Chapter Five

Early the next morning, I stood in the driveway admiring the way the sun gleamed off the freshly waxed hood of my truck. The weather was gorgeous. Dressed in a bathing-suit top with shorts, I could feel the hot sun on my bare shoulders. It had been a long time since I'd given my truck so much attention. I bent down to scrub the dirty whitewall tires.

"What's the occasion?" Mo asked from the front porch.

"Oh, no reason," I replied innocently. There was no way I was going to tell her I was cleaning and scrubbing my pickup in the hope that Jason might need a ride home again tonight after the show.

"My car could use a wash, too," she said with a grin, and went back into the house.

I stood up to rest my back a little. Scrubbing whitewalls was definitely a chore. With a sigh, I turned back to the job at hand. Dipping my scrub brush into the soapy water, I bent down again to attack the dirty tire. If Jason noticed, it would be worth every second of effort.

When I was finally finished, I dumped the bucket, stashed it in the garage, and ran inside to put on my running shoes and a shirt.

Running always made me feel great. As my feet hit the pavement in a rhythmic motion, my thoughts drifted to Jason. We were actually going to go on a date—well, kind of a date. He had said he'd take me for pizza. I pictured the two of us seated in Antonio's elegant Italian restaurant. Jason would order in Italian, and hold my hand across the table. . . .

After a while, my left leg started to cramp a little, so I headed back toward my street, and almost bumped into the mailman, who was on his way to my house. He handed me our mail. "Here you go, Krista. You can save me the trip up to your porch."

I sorted through the mail as I went inside, and was delighted to find a letter from Beth.

Out of breath, I dumped the rest of the mail on the coffee table, plopped down on the couch, and ripped open Beth's letter. She had written to me on some sort of weird stationery with leaf prints all over it. *Must be a camp project, I thought.*

Dear Krista,

Camp is a drag. I love being outdoors, but the food is horrible and the kids are driving me crazy. Ten-year-olds can be a real nightmare! One counselor got tied up and another found honey under her bed, complete with a long trail of ants. I don't think I'd want to be a counselor—being an assistant is bad enough. It's like being a full-time baby-sitter. This is definitely not my idea of fun.

The theater sounds so wonderful! I can't believe everything is working out so well for you and Jason. I must admit he's pretty gorgeous. You haven't said much about Trevor. How is he doing?

The next camp session is supposed to be much smaller, so it should be easier to handle (I hope!). There's even been some talk of sending some of us ACs home early, and if that happens, I'll be the first to volunteer. Maybe I'll see you soon. Cross your fingers!

Love,
Beth

It would be absolutely super if Beth could come home early. Maybe she could see the musical and meet Jason. I'd have my best friend back, and someone to talk to about him.

That night I stood backstage at the theater, watching Jason from the wings. He looked super in the tuxedo he wore for the finale. Tonight's performance was going smoothly and Jason, of course, was outstanding. I hadn't been able to talk to him before the show to see if he wanted me to take him home, but his car had not been in the parking lot when I arrived, so the odds were in my favor.

After the final curtain, Mr. Colby dismissed the cast. Then he and Penny directed a few comments to the backstage crew. I watched anxiously as Jason headed for the dressing rooms, thinking that if they didn't hurry up, I'd miss my chance to offer him a ride.

"Krista, did you get that?" Penny asked, making me jump.

"Uh—no," I mumbled. "I'm sorry. Could you repeat it?"

"The chairs for the Soda Shoppe scene need to be more stage left, because they're getting in the way of the dancers," she said. "Look for the masking tape marks on the floor."

I nodded, then looked back toward the dressing rooms, but Jason had disappeared.

After Mr. Colby and Penny had finished, I ran to get my things from the greenroom, then waited outside Jason's dressing room. He *had* to come out soon! When he finally emerged, carrying a bag, I said, "Hey, Jason, great show!"

"Thanks, Krista." He grinned at me. "Don't worry—I haven't forgotten about the pizza I promised you."

"Oh, I wasn't even thinking about . . ."

"How about tomorrow? We could grab a bite to eat before the show. Say around six?"

"Okay," I said. "Sounds great." I hoped he might say something about needing a ride, but he didn't. It looked like I would have to come right out and ask him. "I was wondering . . ." I began.

"Jason!" Trina called impatiently.

"Just a minute, Krista," he said, and went over to join her.

Pulling a notebook out of my bag, I paged through it, trying to watch them out of the corner of my eye.

A moment later, Jason called, "I'll talk to you tomorrow, Krista. I'm hitching a ride with Trina—I haven't gotten a new tire yet."

"Okay," I called back, trying to hide my disappointment. I stood there watching as Jason turned and walked toward the back door with Trina firmly latched on to his elbow.

"Rats!" I muttered when they had gone. So much for my perfect opportunity to be alone with Jason. Now he would be driving home in Trina's car while I drove home alone in my freshly washed pickup.

But the thought of our dinner date tomorrow quickly changed my mood. I would be with Jason, and she wouldn't. Again I thought about Antonio's. It was the perfect place for a first date—so romantic! How would I ever wait until then?

Somehow I managed. Pulling into the theater parking lot the following night at six, I saw that Jason's car was not there yet. I was so nervous that my hands were sweating. Maybe he still hadn't gotten his new tire. Maybe he wasn't going to show up. Maybe something better had come along . . . Finally, after what seemed like hours, I saw the blue Camaro swing into the lot, and I heaved a huge sigh of relief.

"Sorry I'm late," Jason said, jumping out of his car. He was wearing jeans and a T-shirt. Suddenly I felt very overdressed in my miniskirt and heels. "I had to run an errand for my parents." He walked over to my truck. "Do you mind if we take yours? I've always wanted to drive one of these things."

"Uh—sure. Hop in," I said, sliding over into the passenger seat and stuffing the bag that held my black stage clothes behind it.

He got in the driver's side. "Let's zip on over to Pizza Hut, okay? They get you in and out real fast."

Pizza Hut! My dream date was a trip to *Pizza Hut*?

A few minutes later we sat down at a little table in the back of the pizza place. It wasn't a very romantic setting, but Jason's deep blue eyes made me melt inside. I had to concentrate hard on what he was saying, or I'd have gotten lost in those eyes.

As I moved my foot under the table, I could feel it touch Jason's, and my stomach did a series of little flips. I wondered if he felt the same way. Boldly I rubbed my foot against his.

"Krista, I'm going to grab some napkins for us before the pizza gets here," Jason said.

I hated the thought of his foot moving from mine. But to my astonishment, when he got up, his foot *didn't* move. I looked under the table, and discovered I had been playing footsie with the table leg! I could feel my cheeks turn deep red.

"You okay, Krista?" Jason asked, dropping a fistful of napkins on the table.

"Fine," I said as I tucked my feet underneath my chair.

I was glad when the pizza arrived. Eating helped to take my mind off my romantic encounter with the table leg.

"Hey, I'm really looking forward to the cast picnic," Jason said between bites. "It should be a lot of fun. You are going, aren't you?"

He caught me midmouthful, and it took me a minute to swallow. "What picnic?" I asked.

"I'm surprised you haven't heard. Colby promised us a picnic a week from next Saturday. He even said he'd throw in a couple of six-foot sub sandwiches if the show keeps going well. Mark it on your calendar."

"Oh, I will," I told him eagerly. Perhaps he would ask me to go with him. I'd love to see the look on Trina's face if Jason and I showed up at the picnic together.

Jason glanced at his watch. "Oh, wow! Look at the time! We're going to be big-time late." Grabbing the last couple of slices, he bolted for the door, pausing just long enough to pay the bill, and I hurried after him. A moment later we were in the truck, heading for the theater. Jason pulled into the parking lot and jumped out.

"Krista, you're a doll! Thanks for letting me drive the truck, and for giving me a hand last week," he said as he jumped out of the truck, sprinting for the theater door.

Boy, our so-called date hadn't turned out

at all like I'd planned! There had been no quiet drive in Jason's Camaro, no romantic dinner at Antonio's, and no farewell kiss— just Pizza Hut and a friendly table leg!

Feeling depressed, I grabbed my bag of black clothes and headed for the theater. It was impossible to walk quickly in the high heels I'd worn for this special occasion, so after stumbling twice, I took the shoes off and ran across the parking lot in my bare feet.

Hurrying into the greenroom, I saw that the clock said seven-thirty—a half hour late for our call.

"Well, don't you look fantastic!" Trevor said as I came in. He was sitting on the sofa in his black attire. I couldn't tell whether he was teasing or serious. Trevor serious? No way! He was definitely teasing. "You didn't have to dress up just for me—I think you look great all in black," he added.

I struck an exaggerated pose. "I thought my backstage costume could use a little pizzazz."

"You're right. And those shoes are so practical," he said, looking at the high heels in my hand. "You must wear them to the cast picnic. I insist."

His sarcasm was too much. I gave him a whack with my bag. "Are you sure this picnic includes us lowly stagehands?"

"Lowly!" Trevor said melodramatically. "Without us, there is but a dark empty stage surrounding the actors. *We* provide the props that create the illusion of time and place. *We* are the backbone of the whole performance!" He was about to continue, but Penny's voice from onstage interrupted his speech. "Trevoooorr!"

"As much as I like the feminine look, maybe you'd better find something exciting in good old basic black."

I patted my bag and curtsied. "Your wish is my command, sir."

"I'll tell Penny you're checking costumes." He winked and left.

Costumes! Oh, no! I had forgotten to iron Trina's cape! She'd be furious!

I did a quick change and dashed down the hall to the costume room. There was the cape, crumpled in a ball. With a sigh, I plugged in the iron. After all, this was part of my job.

While the iron heated, I looked around the costume room, remembering Trevor quoting Shakespeare on my first day at the theater. He was hilarious, and so easy to talk to. I wished I could talk to Jason the way I could talk to Trevor. Somehow, I always felt so uneasy with Jason.

The iron hissed, letting me know it was ready for action. Maybe I'd have better luck at the cast picnic. It would be a change of pace, away from the theater.

With that thought in mind, I began to press Trina's cape. I was starting to feel a little better. After all, the picnic was only a week away. . . .

Chapter Six

The day of the picnic was perfect—sunny and warm but with a light breeze so you didn't broil. Pulling into the parking lot in my pickup, I could hear shouts and laughter coming from the park behind the theater.

Trevor pulled up in the space next to me and got out of his bug. "Hey, cool! I'm close for a jump-start later! This old thing still isn't feeling too well." He patted the front fender of his car affectionately.

As we walked to the park together, I looked around for Jason, hoping he wouldn't think Trevor was my date or anything. But I didn't see him anywhere, so when Trevor started talking with one of the dancers, I slipped away to search for Jason and finally spotted him deep in conversation with another actor.

Joining a group of girls nearby, I made sure to stay in Jason's vicinity just in case he felt a sudden urge to walk over and kiss me—I mean, *talk* to me.

A few minutes later, the sub man came. Trevor and a couple other guys ran to give him a hand with the enormous sandwiches. They held the subs high over their heads and began running around and dodging each other like maniacs.

"He's resurfacing, sir! Time to dive, dive, dive!" Trevor yelled. The way they were carrying on, I was sure our lunch was history, but at last the subs made a safe landing on a picnic table under some trees.

People pounced on the sandwiches as if they hadn't eaten in weeks. I fought my way through the wild tangle of arms, hands, and plates, and managed to escape with a hefty chunk of sub.

"Aren't these terrific?" I said to Sarah, one of the dancers, who sat down beside me on the grass.

"Ummm." She nodded in agreement as she munched. "I think Molly already went back for seconds."

Molly was the lead dancer, and she looked the part—tall and willowy. I could see her long ponytail bobbing over at the picnic table. Molly soon joined us with another plateful, and the three of us chatted while we ate our lunch. When we had finished, I was so stuffed that all I wanted to do was stretch out in the shade and digest, but Trevor had other ideas.

"Okay, everyone, gather round, gather round," he shouted, herding everybody into a group. "As I'm sure you know, a picnic just isn't a picnic without games. So we're going to have a variety of races, starting with a sack race, then a wheelbarrow race, and finally a three-legged race."

"Are there prizes?" someone yelled.

"Oh, sure—*fabulous* prizes. Such fabulous prizes that I dare not mention them at this moment for fear you might all pass out!"

Trevor was in charge of the games, of course, and he gave a running play-by-play of each event. In the sack race, Molly and I bumped into each other and tumbled to the ground, laughing so hard that we couldn't get up. I sat out the wheelbarrow race because I was still recovering from the sack race. The last race was the three-legged. I looked eagerly for Jason, hoping he would ask me to be his partner, but I saw him tying his leg to Trina's. Great. Just what I needed.

"What about you, Trevor?" someone yelled.

"I'm the master of ceremonies," Trevor replied loftily.

"What's the matter, Trev? Afraid we'll beat you?" Jason called out.

Trevor turned to me. "Come on, Krista! Let's show 'em how this race is done." Before I could object, he had tied our ankles together. We took a couple of practice steps, then joined the others at the starting line.

"On your mark . . . Get set . . . Go!" shouted Mr. Colby.

Trevor and I took off in a three-legged sprint and easily pulled ahead of the hobbling pack.

"You're pretty good," Trevor panted.

"I run track," I said, trying to concentrate on not falling all over our feet. As we neared the finish line, we fell out of step. Trevor's foot, the one that was tied to mine, jerked forward a beat too soon and it threw me off balance. I knew we were going to fall, and we did. Now the two of us were tangled together.

"Crawl!" Trevor hollered.

So we scrambled forward on all fours, arms and legs going all different directions. We finally *rolled* across the finish line, but we were still ahead of the others.

By this time we were both laughing so hard that tears were streaming down our cheeks. When we finally stopped laughing, we had to take off our shoes to get our feet untangled. After a triumphant "high-five" and a shaky rendition of "We Are the Champions," Trevor and I were awarded candy bars by Mr. Colby, and the races were over.

Sitting down in the shade, I pulled off my socks. The cool grass felt so good on my hot feet! I was wiggling my bare toes when to my delight, Jason walked over to where I was sitting. He was still out of breath. "Trevor just told me you're a track star," he said, grinning. "No wonder you guys left us all eating your dust! But your finish needs a little work." Jason winked at me. "Next time, Krista, it's you and me, okay?"

"We'll see about that," I teased. "If there *is* a next time." Oh, if he only knew how much I had wanted to be his partner! The way he said "you and me" made me feel warm inside.

Suddenly somebody screamed. "*Ahhh!* Help! Help!" Trina was jumping up and down, waving her arms wildly as she ran from the picnic table. "Get it away from me! *Help!*"

Several of the kids ran over to her, trying to figure out what was going on. She was really acting crazy, and that was completely out of character for pseudosophisticated Trina.

I glanced at the picnic table where she had been sitting—*bees!* Trina obviously had a bad case of the "Beth Bee Syndrome." There were a couple of the fuzzy little creatures crawling around the leftovers, and as I walked over to the table and brushed them away, I noticed that there were a lot more of them flying all over the place. I realized these were

71

not just your usual backyard bees. They were angry yellow jackets!

Then something tickled my foot. Looking down, I saw a flash of black and yellow between two of my toes. I reached down to brush the bee away, but not in time. I felt an excruciating pain between my toes, and another in the heel of my other foot. I desperately wanted to sit down, but I was afraid I would land on another yellow jacket. Finally, I hobbled away from the picnic table and collapsed on the ground.

"Krista, are you all right?" Sarah asked, looking down at me.

"The little suckers got me on both feet, but I think I'm going to live," I managed to reply. My feet were throbbing and already beginning to swell. For the first time I understood why people hated bees and wasps so much!

Everyone crowded around, forgetting all about Trina.

Trevor elbowed his way to the front of the pack and bent down to look at my puffy feet. "We need some ice," he called out.

"There isn't any more—some of the kids were having an ice fight earlier," Molly said.

Marcie Lopez, the girl from my algebra class, shrugged. "How were we supposed to know she'd go and get stung—*twice*?" She flipped her braided hair and hurried off to join Trina, who was sulking under a tree.

"I'll find some," Trevor said, and took off toward the parking lot.

My feet were stinging and aching so much that I closed my eyes for a second. When I opened them, I saw Jason kneeling beside me.

"I know just the thing," he said.

Before I knew what was happening, he had picked me up and was carrying me over to the stream. My gallant knight had rescued me after the attack, and swept me away in his arms! How completely romantic!

We reached the stream, and Jason set me down gently on the bank. "The cold water will help," he assured me as I stuck my feet into the icy stream. He was right—it did feel good, numbing my aches and pains.

"Better?" Jason asked, sitting down next to me.

"Lots. Thank you," I said.

He smiled. "No problem. From the way you tackled those bees, I guess you're not afraid of them, huh?"

"I *wasn't*. I've never been stung before," I confessed, wiggling my toes in the water. I really couldn't think of anything else to say. As we sat in silence, I tried to think of something. Jason might leave if he thought I was boring.

"The play sure has been going well," I said finally.

He nodded, and then looked intently at me. I could feel his eyes pierce right through me. It was as if he were looking into my soul! He could probably even read my mind, which was silently screaming, "I am crazy about you, Jason!"

He moved closer to me. Maybe he *had* read my mind! My heart raced. I could hardly breathe. He was so close, close enough to kiss me. Maybe he *was* going to kiss me! What should I do? Should I keep my eyes open or close them if he kissed me? Some people say it's better with your eyes closed, but others say they like to see the moment as well as feel it.

Jason moved even closer.

This was it! This was the moment! I raised my face to his and slowly closed my eyes . . .

Nothing happened. Or had I missed it? I quickly opened my eyes again to find Jason staring at me.

"Are you okay?" he asked. "I was just thinking that your face looks a little red and puffy. Maybe you're having an allergic reaction and we should get you to a doctor."

"I'm fine," I mumbled. *Red and puffy!* Boy, did I feel stupid! I wanted to crawl under the nearest rock and hide for all eternity.

"Are you sure you're okay?"

I tried to speak but nothing came out, so I just nodded.

Jason stood up. "Maybe you need a drink. I'll get you some lemonade if there's any left." He hurried off in the direction of the picnic table.

I had made a complete fool of myself. At least nobody else knew—nobody but me, anyway. I tried to laugh. You have to be able to laugh at yourself when you do stupid things. I must have read that in a book somewhere. Well, whoever said it was right. Thinking about how silly I must have looked sitting there with my face turned upward and my eyes closed, I giggled a little.

"What's so funny? Did I miss the punch line?" It was Trevor's voice behind me. He had a bag of ice in one arm and a large thermos in the other. "We're all out of cups, so I brought the whole jug. Jason was going to do it but Colby grabbed him, so I volunteered to bring refreshment to our wounded." He set the bag of ice down next to me, then held the thermos up over my head. "Open wide."

"Trevor! Don't even *think* about it!" I cried, laughing.

He gave me an innocent look. "What do you think I'm going to do—drown you?" He tipped my head back and I reluctantly opened my mouth.

"Hmm. I see a lot of fillings in there," Trevor said.

Then he turned on the spigot, and lemonade flowed into my mouth—well, most of it went into my mouth. The rest dribbled down my chin, my neck, and even into my ears.

"Trevor!" I laughed as I wiped my face. "If I were a walking woman, you would be a dead man!"

He grinned. "Feeling refreshed, are we?"

Kicking my feet, I splashed water all over him, giggling as the shocked look on his face melted into laughter.

"Yes, I do believe we are *both* feeling refreshed now." Trevor sat down on a rock, the bag of melting ice between us. "How are your feet?"

I wiggled my toes again. "Pretty good, I think—I can't really feel them anymore. The stream is pretty cold."

"Then I guess you didn't need any ice."

"No, but thanks for getting it."

He smiled. "My pleasure."

Ripping open the bag of ice, he threw a cube into the stream. It bobbed up and down as the water carried it away. Then I tossed one.

We sat and threw ice cubes like that until the last one was gone, laughing like a couple of little kids.

"Ready to go?" Trevor asked at last.

I nodded. "Sure."

"Will the feet hold out?"

"No problem." I took my wrinkled feet out of the water and tried to stand up, then grimaced. They weren't as numb as I had thought they were.

"Looks like it's time for a piggyback ride," Trevor said. "Hop on, gimp." He bent over and pointed to his back.

I weighed the options—walking on my sore feet, or trusting Trevor not to drop me. Trevor won; my poor feet were killing me.

He took off like a racehorse out of the starting gate. It was a rough ride as we bounded up to the picnic site. When we got there, Mr. Colby had gathered everyone together.

"I have an announcement," Mr. Colby said. "As you all know, Lisa Parker will not be here for the last performance—she has to leave for her great-grandmother's hundredth birthday celebration in New York. What you *don't* know is that Gretchen Houser, Lisa's understudy, quit last night. This means I will need a fill-in for Lisa on closing night." A murmur of surprise went through the group. "Listen up!" Mr. Colby went on. "Any chorus member may try out for the part. I'm going to hold an audition next Wednesday night after the show. I know it's a lot of work for just *one* performance, but be sure you know all Lisa's lines and blocking."

"Excuse me." Trevor's hand shot up. "Are only chorus members allowed to try out?"

Mr. Colby laughed and shook his head. "No, any member of the company is eligible. Trevor, if *you* would like to audition for the role of Bernard's youngest sister, go right ahead. You'd look super in a ruffled pinafore!"

Everyone laughed, but I wouldn't have put it past Trevor to do just that.

Mr. Colby's announcement signaled the end of the picnic. As the kids started to leave, they were all buzzing with excitement about the tryout.

I found my socks and running shoes where I had left them. Carefully I slipped them on. The shoes felt a little tight, but I wasn't going to take the chance of stepping on another yellow jacket.

I looked around for Jason and saw him talking to Trina. After the stupid way I'd acted that afternoon, I didn't feel like waiting for him, so I turned and limped toward the parking lot.

Trevor fell in step beside me. "So when do you want to start rehearsing for the tryout?"

I stopped short and stared at him. *"What?"*

"The audition. You'd be perfect for Lisa's part."

I laughed and started limping again. "Trevor, there is no way I am trying out for a musical!"

"Why not?" He caught up with me easily.

"Number one, I haven't been onstage since fifth grade, and number two, I sing like a sick cow."

"Come on, Krista—you know cows can't sing."

"Exactly, and neither can I."

Trevor persisted. "It's easy." He began to sing a scale. "Do, re, mi . . ."

I sang the same notes in my worst possible voice: "Not, a, chance . . ."

Trevor rolled his eyes. "Okay, you made your point. But you could mouth the songs. The part of Cece doesn't have any solos. She just sings with the chorus."

We argued back and forth until we got to the parking lot.

"How about a jump-start?" I asked, changing the subject.

Trevor raised an eyebrow, but allowed the subject to be changed. "A jump would be super."

We had this down to a science by now. Trevor grabbed the cables, I popped the hoods, he hooked up the cables to the batteries, and I hopped into my truck. We revved our engines, and Trevor's bug sputtered to life.

I jumped out and unhooked the cables. "We're pros," I said, handing them to Trevor. "We do the fastest jump-start in town."

He grinned. "Remember, practice makes

perfect. And *you* are going to practice like crazy for the tryout next week." He drove off before I could start protesting again. There was no way I was going to try out for a part in the show!

Chapter Seven

But somehow, with Trevor, things didn't always go the way I planned, which was how I ended up on the stage the next afternoon with a script in my hand.

"Oh, forget it! This is impossible!" I groaned as I plopped down on the floor. Trevor and I had been rehearsing a scene for the audition, and it was obvious to me that even this bit part was out of my league. Trevor had said it would be simple, but acting was not as easy as he made it sound.

"Come on. You can do it." Trevor picked up his script and went through the dialogue again, reading both parts. "See? Piece of cake."

"Okay, I'll try it one more time." I stood up, but before I could start, I heard Trina's voice calling from the wings, "Don't bother! My friend Marcie is trying out, and she's sure to get the part."

I clenched my fists. "Oooh, Trina makes me so *mad!*"

"Mad enough to try out?" Trevor looked me right in the eye.

I hesitated, then said, "As a matter of fact, yes. But I'm *not* going to rehearse here where everyone who wanders into the theater can watch." Grabbing my purse, I marched off-stage and out to the parking lot, with Trevor right on my heels.

"Oh, good thinking. The parking lot is real private," he said, laughing.

I shook my car keys at him. "Not here, dummy. I live only a couple miles away. We can practice at my house."

He threw up his hands. "Teasing, just teasing."

For once his bug didn't need a jump, but it did sputter a lot. When we got to my house, I leaned out the window and motioned for Trevor to pull into the driveway. It would be easier for a roll-start later.

"So this is where you live." He gave my house the once-over.

I clapped my hands briskly. "No time to ponder. It's time to practice, practice!" He shrugged and followed me inside.

"Krista, is that you?" Mo called from the kitchen.

"Yeah, it's me . . ."

"Good! You want to clean up the mess you left in the bathroom this morning?" she said, coming into the hall with Bobby right behind her. My face flushed. "Oh—you have company."

"Mo, this is my friend Trevor, from the theater," I said.

Bobby's eyes widened. "Oh, Krista's got a boyfriend!"

I shot him a dirty look. Little brothers can be so embarrassing!

"Krista's got a boyfriend, Krista's got a boyfriend," Bobby chanted over and over.

"Bobby," I said impatiently, "Trevor is *not* my boyfriend."

He gave me a superinnocent look. "He's a boy. And he's your friend. So he's your boyfriend."

I turned to Mo for help.

"Bobby, quit teasing your sister," she said firmly, but it was obvious that she was amused by the whole situation.

"Trevor and I will be up in the TV room," I said. Pushing Trevor toward the stairs, I added to Bobby, "And you aren't invited."

As soon as we got to the TV room, I closed the door behind us. "He's such a pest!" I said.

"Nah, Bobby's cool."

"You obviously don't have a younger brother," I chided.

"You're right. I have two older sisters."

I pointed a finger at him. "You probably were a Bobby when you were that age."

"Who, me?" Trevor said, pretending to be amazed. Then he shuffled through the blocking notes he had copied from Penny's prompt book. "Okay—rehearsal time."

Feeling suddenly insecure, I said, "Do you think this is even worth going through? I don't think there's much of a chance for me."

"Chill out, Krista. The character is only in three scenes and she doesn't do any dancing. All you need to do is learn the lines, remember the blocking, and sing the songs." He corrected himself. "*Mouth* the songs."

"Easy for you to say!"

"True," he agreed. "Now let's get to work."

We went through each scene, and Trevor showed me exactly what Bernard's sister would be doing. As I practiced the lines, he played all the other parts. After the seventh or eighth time, I began to get the hang of it.

"This isn't so hard," I said.

Trevor smiled. "You're catching on pretty quick."

There was a knock on the door, and Mo poked her head in. "Can you stay for dinner, Trevor?"

Dinner? I looked at my watch. We had been working for three hours!

Trevor looked at me; I nodded. Turning

back to my mom, he said, "I'd love to, Mrs. Winters."

"What are we having, Mo?" I asked.

"Hamburgers and corn on the cob," she said, and disappeared.

"Mo?" Trevor looked at me, puzzled. "As in Curly, Larry, and . . . ?"

"No, it's short for Mother. But I'll tell her you thought she was one of the Three Stooges," I joked. We moved the furniture back into place and headed downstairs. "I don't know about you, but I'm starved."

"I need to call home," Trevor said as we came into the kitchen.

I pointed to the phone on the wall and he began to dial. I noticed that Mo had set the table with her prettiest place mats and fancy dishes.

"What's the occasion?" my dad asked, joining us. Mo nudged him and shot a look over at Trevor. "Oh, a young man," Dad said, raising his eyebrows.

"Dad, Trevor is a *friend*," I informed him.

Trevor hung up the phone. "No problem. My mom says to thank you for inviting me."

I introduced Trevor to my dad. They shook hands, and the three of us sat down to eat. A moment later, Bobby came thundering down the stairs to join us. Mo served the hamburgers on the good plates as if they were filet mignon. Everyone's manners were impeccable, including Bobby's. This was really bizarre!

"So, Trevor, you work at the theater with Krista," Mo commented politely. "Are you an actor?"

"No, not this summer. I work backstage, getting the props ready and moving the scenery."

"Where do you go to school?" Dad asked.

"Kennedy High."

The interview continued. Mo's turn this time. "How old are you, Trevor?"

"Sixteen."

My parents nodded at each other and smiled.

"So, Trevor, do you like bugs?" Bobby chimed in.

Trevor laughed. "Yeah, they're pretty cool, Bobby. As a matter of fact, I own one—it's parked in your driveway."

The stuffy atmosphere had been broken. The rest of the meal was normal—eating, talking, and laughing.

After dinner, Trevor helped me do the dishes. "Boy, your dad was sure grilling me," he said. "You'd think we were going out or something."

"Oh, he's just interested in all my friends." I laughed, brushing off the "going out" comment. When we finished the dishes, I walked Trevor to the front door.

"Dinner was great. Practice was great. I'm outta here," he said.

I smiled. "Thanks for helping me out. I really appreciate it."

"Hey, keep up the good work, and you'll blow Marcie away."

I gave him a thumbs-up, he rolled his car backward down the drive, and the little bug sputtered away.

It had been a fun afternoon. But the *real* fun would start if I could land that part. I'd be onstage with Jason—we'd have to rehearse together—and maybe he'd really notice me once I was an actress, not just a stagehand.

All week long Trevor and I spent every afternoon rehearsing. I practiced Cece's lines until I could say them right along with Lisa as she played the part onstage.

On Wednesday night, Mr. Colby told the cast and crew that all those who wanted to try out were to meet in the auditorium as soon as the show was over.

After the final curtain call, I rushed to the costume room to change out of my black clothes, and slipped into my blue sundress. I may have looked silly wearing it as a stagehand, but now it was appropriate for the role of Bernard's sister.

I checked my appearance one last time in

the mirror, crossed my fingers, and hurried to the auditorium. Six other girls were sitting in the front row, still in costume. Mr. Colby was standing in front of the group—and sitting behind him on the apron of the stage was Jason. I froze. I couldn't do it with Jason watching! What if he laughed at me? I turned and started back through the door to safety, only to run right into Trevor.

"And where do you think you're going?" he asked, putting a hand on my bare shoulder.

"I can't do it! Jason is out there, and I can't do it in front of him," I wailed.

"You did it in front of me," Trevor pointed out.

"I know. It's just—different."

He gave me a questioning look.

"I mean, well, Jason's a real actor and I'm not and he might laugh, and—well, I just can't. Okay?"

"*Not* okay." He folded his arms. "The ones who *are* going to laugh are Trina and Marcie if you wimp out."

He had a point. I couldn't stand the thought of Trina's ridicule. "You're right, Trevor. I guess I'm just being weird." Taking a deep breath, I turned, yanked the door open, and walked back into the auditorium.

I joined the other girls, making it seven who were trying out for the part. I saw Marcie turn and whisper something to the blonde sitting next to her, and they both snickered. I knew I shouldn't let it bother me, but it did.

"Okay, girls," Mr. Colby said. "We'll do act one, scene five between Bernard and his sister Cece. You all should know the lines by now and have a good handle on the blocking. Who wants to go first?"

Of course Marcie was the first to volunteer. With a toss of her long, dark hair, she walked up onto the stage and went through the scene perfectly with Jason. She didn't miss a single cue or flub a single line. I could swear she smirked at me when the scene was over. The next five girls were pretty good, too. I thought about trying to slip out again, but I was afraid that Trevor was still guarding the door.

"Krista?" Mr. Colby said at last, looking over at me.

Well, here goes nothing, I thought, as I slowly went up the steps to the stage. I had never in my whole life been so nervous, not even when I played the Scarecrow in fifth grade. Taking a deep breath, I moved into place, silently telling myself, "You *can* do this. You *can!*"

Jason said his first line: "Cece, I told you not to follow me here!"

My mind went absolutely blank. I couldn't remember a single word. I just stood there saying nothing and looking stupid.

"Krista?" Mr. Colby said gently.

"Uh—I wasn't ready. Could we start again?" I wiped my sweaty hands on my skirt.

"All right. From the top," he said. I could hear the skepticism in his voice. Would I just make a bigger fool of myself by trying again?

"Cece, I told you not to follow me here!"

This time everything clicked. The lines came back to me, and I slipped right into the role. Jason and I bantered back and forth with the dialogue, having a good time with it.

"Okay, super!" Mr. Colby interrupted in the middle of the scene. I wished he hadn't stopped us—I was ready to do the whole script. It was actually a lot of fun.

"Everyone up onstage." The six other girls joined us. "Considering the time frame," Mr. Colby said, "I have to make a quick decision. You were all terrific, but one of you showed a special flair. Krista Winters, the part is yours."

I let out a little gasp. I wanted to jump up and down, but I didn't. "Thank you," I said softly.

Karen, one of the other girls who had tried out, gave me a big smile. "Congratulations, Krista. You were really good."

"Good job! Congrats," several of the others added as they left the stage, but Marcie just scowled and didn't say a word.

Jason walked over to me. "You were great,"

he said, smiling. "I'm glad Marcie didn't get the part—she can be a real pain sometimes." He draped an arm around my shoulders. "Let's meet here tomorrow afternoon and run through the scenes a few times. You probably know them pretty well, but it never hurts to be extra sure. Then on Friday we can practice in costume."

"Sounds great," I said. "What time?"

"How about three o'clock? We can work for a few hours, then get a bite to eat before the show."

I nodded. "Perfect!" Absolutely perfect. We'd practice, we'd eat. Who knows—maybe we'd even fall in love!

"See you then." He let me go and took off backstage.

I walked to the back of the auditorium, and sat down in the last row, gazing at the stage. On Saturday night, I would be up there with Jason. This was the best day of my life! It was definitely something to celebrate, and I wished Beth were there. It's kind of tough to celebrate all by yourself.

"Krista?" Trevor came onstage, looking around. "Krista!" he called again.

"Hey you, I'm out here!" I called back.

"Well, get up here. I understand we have some celebrating to do!"

Laughing, I ran down the aisle. I was so lucky to have a friend like Trevor!

Chapter Eight

"I can't believe I made it!" I exclaimed as I came onto the stage.

"Mr. Colby said you were super," Trevor told me.

"I did it! I can't believe I did it!" I cried, spinning around in circles.

"Obviously he didn't ask you to sing."

I stopped twirling and gave him a playful punch. "I thought we were supposed to be celebrating."

"Stay right where you are." Trevor disappeared backstage, reappearing in a moment with a bottle and two glasses. "I brought some sparkling apple cider, just in case." He popped the plastic cork, which landed somewhere near the fourth row. "This occasion deserves a toast." He filled our glasses, and motioned for me to sit on the edge of the stage.

Trevor sat next to me and raised his glass. "To the thrill of victory, and"—a big smile spread across his face—"to the agony of Marcie's and Trina's defeat." Our glasses clinked, and we each took a sip. The bubbles from the cider tickled my nose.

Trevor set down his glass. "I'm really proud of you, Krista." He looked into my eyes, his gaze searching for something. But what? I was confused. "I knew you could do it." He took my hand in his. What was going on?

Before I could answer my own question, Trevor was leaning toward me. The next few seconds seemed to pass in slow motion. Putting his hand under my chin, he tipped my face up to his. Closer and closer he came, until he finally pressed his lips to mine. My eyes closed automatically as I savored the kiss. . . .

Wait a minute! My eyes popped open. I was kissing *Trevor*!

"What are you doing?" I squawked and jerked away, knocking over his glass.

"Well, some people call it kissing." Trevor smiled, ignoring the puddle of cider.

"But *why* were you kissing me?" I demanded.

He shrugged. "At the time, it seemed like the right thing to do."

"Well, it wasn't! Just don't do it again, okay?"

"I'm sorry, Krista. I guess I rushed you a little bit."

"I . . . I just don't like you in that way," I mumbled. "I thought we were friends."

"We *are* friends. I just thought . . ."

"I'm going to be rehearsing with Jason," I interrupted, "and . . . well, I'm just . . ."

Trevor nodded. "I see. So you're interested in Jason?"

I looked away. "Well, I *would* like to get to know him a little bit better."

"You and every other girl in the cast," Trevor said bitterly.

Glaring at him, I blurted out, "You're just mad because I like him better than you!"

"Oh, I didn't know that you despise my company."

"That's not what I said. What I meant was—"

This time Trevor interrupted. "Look, Krista, I read you loud and clear. I'm outta here."

All I could do was watch him go. He had taken everything I'd said the wrong way. Or maybe I had said it all the wrong way. Whatever, it didn't matter now. He was gone.

The spilled cider was soaking into my dress. I felt miserable—make that *wet* and miserable.

I arrived at the theater early the next afternoon for my first rehearsal with Jason. Seeing Trevor's car in the parking lot gave me an uncomfortable feeling. But thoughts of yesterday faded quickly when I saw Jason waiting for me outside.

"Ready to go to work?" he asked.

"Sure am!" I followed him into the theater.

"I asked Lisa Parker to stop by and work with us—I thought it would be helpful. She'll be over in about an hour."

Darn! Now I'd have to share Jason again—but on second thought, it would be good to get some pointers from the girl I'd be replacing.

Once onstage, Jason moved some of the props around to set up the scene we'd be practicing. "I guess it'll be quite a change for you, going from stagehand to performer."

"Yeah, I guess so." I didn't really know what else to say, so I just sort of stood there feeling awkward.

"Have you done much theater before?" Jason asked.

"Well, not really." Another giant pause.

"Well, I guess we'd better get started," he said at last. So much for small talk. I must have been making quite an impression. Why couldn't I ever think of anything interesting to say to him?

"We'll start with scene three, the one with just Bernard and Cece. Then scene five. We can walk through the finale, but it will be easier with everyone here."

"Sounds good," I said.

The first scene went really well—I did every-thing right. The next didn't go so well. In the middle of scene five, Bernard was supposed to put his arm around his little sister and give her a kiss on the forehead. But each time we got close to that part, I'd get so ner-vous that I'd blow my lines.

"Okay, I'll get it this time," I assured him after the third try. I *had* to get it this time. I was making a fool of myself. I started the scene off, determined to do it right. As we got closer to the kiss, I started to get the jit-ters, but I concentrated very hard on staying in character.

"Bernard, where have you *been*?" I whim-pered.

"Oh, Cece, it's all right. . . ." Jason put his arm around me. His arm felt so strong as he held me tight. My heart did backflips, and my limbs turned to Jell-O. If only his kiss would land on my lips! I put on Cece's pouty expression. As Jason bent down to kiss my forehead, I looked up . . . and screamed.

A piece of scenery was being lowered right over our heads! Jason quickly let go of me. "What's the big idea?" he yelled.

Alan poked his head in from the wings. "Oh, jeez! I'm sorry—Penny told me the stage was clear."

"Couldn't you *hear* us?" Jason was still upset.

"Hey, I said I'm sorry," Alan repeated.

Trevor came onstage then. "What's going on here?" he said, looking right past me at Jason.

Jason pointed to Alan. "Your stupid crew almost dropped a flat on us!"

"How long will you be working?" Trevor asked.

Jason looked at his watch. "About another hour and a half."

"You got it." Trevor turned and disappeared into the wings. He hadn't even looked at me, hadn't acknowledged my existence. He was obviously still mad from last night. I had to talk to him and explain everything as soon as I got the chance.

Jason shook his head. "Those stagehands can be so dumb sometimes!"

How could he say that? I was a stagehand, or at least, I used to be. Did he think I was dumb, too? My expression must have given away my thoughts, because he said, "I'm sorry, Krista. I didn't mean you, of course."

I relaxed a little, though I didn't appreciate his attitude.

We finished the rest of scene five without any further problems.

Jason patted me on the back. "Nice work, kid."

What did he mean by "kid"? I wasn't that much younger than he was. Well, okay, so I was two years younger. But I hoped he didn't really think of me as just a kid. Maybe he was just staying in character. After all, I was playing his little sister.

"Hey, looking good!" Lisa called from the auditorium. She had slipped into the third row while we were doing the scene. Her brown hair and hazel eyes reminded me of Beth's, but Lisa was at least a foot shorter. "I have a few suggestions though, Krista," she said, coming up onstage. She showed me some different ways to say Cece's lines, and a couple of extra movements to make me seem more childlike.

Lisa worked with Jason and me the next afternoon as well and helped me polish the role, so I had it down pat when Mr. Colby watched our rehearsal on Wednesday.

Working every day onstage with Jason made the week fly by. I hadn't gotten a chance to talk to Trevor, though I tried to. But each time I looked for him, he was gone. Why should that bother me now that I was spending so much time with Jason? I don't know, but it did.

My big night was getting closer and closer, and on Friday, Mr. Colby called a rehearsal of the finale after the show.

Lisa had hung up her costume in the girls' dressing room before she left for the airport. Pinned to the dress was a good-luck note: "Break a leg! Love, Lisa." I picked up the dress, and examined it. It sure looked better on Lisa than it did on a hanger. Orange wasn't my color, but there was nothing I could do about it. I put on a lot of lipstick and blusher so I wouldn't look too washed out, then headed for the stage.

I felt very self-conscious as I walked out among the costumed characters. The stage lights were blinding. I blinked a couple of times, but still only saw spots. Then the music started and everyone scurried to their places.

The scene opened and everything went pretty well. Trina got in my way a few times, but I managed to dodge around her to say my lines. But as the chorus broke into song, Mr. Colby motioned for everyone to stop. He came up onstage and walked over to where I was standing. What was wrong? Had he noticed that I was only mouthing the lyrics?

Mr. Colby looked at me long and hard. Maybe he'd changed his mind. Maybe he'd decided I wasn't right for the part after all. Finally he shook his head. "That dress—the color's all wrong for you." He scratched his chin, then hollered, *"Penny!"* She appeared on cue. "Could you get her another dress? I think there's a blue one on the costume rack."

Carol's curly carrot top emerged from the side curtains. "I know just the dress!"

"Okay, let's take ten minutes," he said to the cast, and then turned to me. "Why don't you go try on the blue dress? But make it fast."

I followed Carol through the backstage area. It was pitch black compared to the bright stage, so I grabbed on to her shirttail and let her guide me through.

"You're doing great," she said as we hurried down the stairs.

"Thanks. Are you guys going to be okay backstage without me?" I asked anxiously.

"Don't worry," she said. "Trevor's pulling double duty tomorrow night. He told Penny and Colby that he'd cover for you if you got the part."

I nodded, realizing that if it wasn't for Trevor, I wouldn't even have tried out for the part, and without his coaching, I never would have gotten it. I wished I had thanked him for everything he'd done for me, but I hadn't, and now he was avoiding me. I wondered if he'd ever talk to me again.

Carol must have read my thoughts. "What's up with you and Trevor, anyway? That is, if you don't mind my asking," she said. "You used to be so tight, and now it's like you two don't know each other. I know it's none of my business, but it's just that Trevor has been so bummed lately."

"I know. I just—don't know," I mumbled.

Carol sighed. "Well, we'd better get you into that dress and back onstage before Colby throws a fit."

The blue dress fit perfectly. Five minutes later, I reappeared onstage in it, and Mr. Colby nodded his approval. He called the cast and started the final scene again. This time Marcie pushed in front of me before each of my lines. I moved around her, and then she shoved a chair in my way. It caught me off guard. I bumped into it and blew my next line.

Trina broke character and put her hands on her hips. "I thought she knew the lines," she snapped at Mr. Colby.

"I do," I told her between clenched teeth.

Marcie glared at me. "Then why don't you say them right?"

"One more time, from the top!" Mr. Colby bellowed. Trina and Marcie flounced back into place, and I heard several of the chorus members grumble as they moved over into position. Everyone was tired and grouchy. This whole thing was turning into a nightmare. Hadn't Mr. Colby noticed what Trina and Marcie were doing? But if I told on them, it would only make things worse.

It was eleven o'clock, and people were antsy to get home. We finally made it through the entire scene without any foul-ups, and Mr. Colby dismissed us. I practically ran off the stage. I'd had more than enough theater to last me the rest of my life! Reaching the greenroom, I plopped down miserably on the old tweed couch.

Then Trevor walked in. He saw me sitting there, and abruptly turned and walked out the other door without a word. I buried my face in my hands. Why was everything such an awful mess?

Half an hour later, I pulled into my driveway. Home at last! Now I could relax, without Trina and Marcie on my back, and Trevor treating me like I had a communicable disease. The theater just wasn't the same without his friendship. I wished everything could be the way it was before he kissed me. Actually, it had been a decent kiss—if only it had been Jason.

As I opened the front door, Mo called from the living room, "Hi, honey. Did you eat? I saved you some dinner."

"Not hungry," I said, walking quickly through the hall, up the stairs, and to my room. I was completely exhausted. Dropping my clothes on the floor, I slipped into my nightshirt and collapsed on the bed. If I made it through tomorrow night, it would be a miracle. I knew I'd feel much better about the whole thing if only Trevor would talk to me and cheer me up. He had always been there to back me up in the past. I couldn't talk to Jason about how nervous and insecure I felt. Heck, I couldn't talk to Jason much about *anything.*

There was a light tap at the door. "Come in," I said halfheartedly. I knew it would be Mo, full of questions.

It was. She sat on the edge of my bed. "Are you all right?" she asked finally.

"I'm okay."

She continued to sit there patiently. I knew she wouldn't leave until she got something out of me, but I didn't feel like volunteering any information.

"Is your part going all right?"

"It's okay." I wrapped my arms around my pillow, then confessed, "It's just everything else that's going wrong. Lousy, in fact."

Mo moved a little closer. "I thought there was something bothering you. You just haven't been your usual happy self lately, Krista. Anything I can do to help?" Her eyes were filled with concern.

"It's just boy stuff." I sighed. "You wouldn't understand."

"You're probably right. I was never your age, and of course there weren't *any* boys around in my day," she teased.

"But this is really *complicated,* Mo."

"Try me."

I took a deep breath and let it out in another huge sigh. Just what I needed—motherly advice on boys. What I *really* needed was Beth. But without her, Mo would have to do. "You met my friend, Trevor," I said. "Well, he's not talking to me anymore, and—"

"Why not?" she interrupted.

I paused. How could I explain this to her? "He's just not. And it really bothers me."

"What happened?" she persisted.

"Trevor kissed me!" I blurted out.

"That's wonderful!" Mo exclaimed.

I groaned. "No, it's not." I might have known she wouldn't understand. I couldn't believe I had even told her. Now she'd probably go and tell the world that her little girl had been kissed!

"I'm sorry, Krista. I thought you liked Trevor," she said quietly.

"I *do* like Trevor. He's my *friend*." I decided to tell her the rest, since I had already told her most of it, and there wasn't anyone else to talk to. "After he kissed me, we kind of had a fight. I think Trevor's mad at me because I like Jason. He hasn't talked to me since."

"Have *you* tried talking to *him*?" Mo asked.

"Well, kind of . . ."

Mo reached out and patted my knee. "Honey, when you pick one boy over another, someone's bound to get hurt. And though you may want to, you can't have them both."

I hugged my pillow tightly. "I know. I'm crazy about Jason. But I miss talking and joking around with Trevor."

"Don't you talk and joke around with Jason?"

I sighed. "No. I'd like to, but it just doesn't seem to work between us. I get all tongue-tied, and he doesn't talk about anything except the show."

"Sounds to me you like Trevor more than Jason," Mo said after a long pause.

"No, I don't," I said quickly.

Mo didn't argue with me. She just smiled a motherly smile and stood up. "You get a good night's sleep, honey. Tomorrow is your big night." She gave me a kiss, then left my room, closing the door behind her.

I turned off the light and tucked my pillow under my head. Obviously Mo didn't understand or else she never would have thought I liked Trevor more than Jason.

Chapter Nine

The following evening, I paused a moment outside the girls' dressing room. Was I ready for this? *Ready as I'll ever be,* I thought, as I pulled open the door. The room was packed and noisy; all twenty girls in the cast were jammed into a room which would comfortably fit ten. They were swarming around the costume rack, trying to find the right costume, coming up with the wrong one, then attacking the rack again, talking and giggling nonstop. I slipped back outside. I was definitely *not* ready to fight that crowd, so I went backstage. It was very quiet. The scenery and props had been set up half an hour before. I wandered over to the prop table, noticing that everything was in its place.

"Hey, you, why aren't you getting ready?" Carol asked, emerging from behind a flat.

"The dressing room's crammed," I told her.

"That's half the fun. I was in *Guys and Dolls* last year, and getting into costume and makeup was my favorite part of it. Don't worry about a thing. We have everything under control." Carol glanced at her watch. "Besides, you don't have much time."

She was right. In only thirty minutes, Mr. Colby would want us all onstage. I hurried back to the dressing room.

The feeding frenzy at the costume rack had cleared out, so I easily found my blue dress. Once in costume, I looked around for an empty seat at the makeup counter. The walls above it were lined with mirrors, each framed by twenty or so light bulbs, some of which were burned out. The other girls were squeezed in three-deep as they tried to apply their makeup.

"Krista, come here," Molly said. She moved over so I could stand beside her.

"It gets pretty crazy, doesn't it?" I said as I wriggled into the tiny space.

"Boy, do you look pale!" Molly exclaimed, looking at my reflection in the mirror. "The stage lights bleach out any bit of tan you have. Did you bring makeup?"

I reached into my purse and pulled out a tube of lipstick and a mascara wand.

She shook her head. "That's not going to cut it. But no problem. You can use mine."

She passed me a tube of tan foundation, and a sponge.

I squeezed out a glob of foundation and spread it on thick with the sponge. It felt as if I were frosting my face like a cake.

Molly started cracking up. "No, Krista, you don't need *that* much!" She took the sponge and expertly fixed my makeup mess, then added rouge, eyeliner, eye shadow, mascara, and lipstick. It sure seemed like a lot of preparation for my one night onstage!

"Ten minutes, then Colby wants to talk to everybody!" Alan warned, poking his head into the dressing room. Everybody immediately moved into fast-forward, and exactly ten minutes later we were all gathered backstage. Mr. Colby went over some last-minute details, then gave us a pep talk. "The auditorium is packed—it's a sellout! Let's give them a show they'll always remember." He smiled. "And have fun with it, kids. It's your last night."

I didn't know about anyone else, but I was suddenly all pumped up, ready to go out and knock 'em dead.

"Good luck!" Carol was at my side. "All the crew is rooting for you, especially Trevor. So break a leg."

"Thanks, Carol." I gave her a hug, and she dashed off. What did she mean, that Trevor was rooting for me? Had he said something to her? Knowing Carol, I decided she was probably just being nice. But I wished Trevor had wished me good luck himself.

"Places, please," Penny said and everyone hurried onstage to their positions for the first scene.

As the two pianos started the overture, I turned into a bundle of nerves even though I wasn't in the opening number. My hands were sweaty, and my stomach was full of butterflies.

The curtains opened on a stage filled with singers and dancers in bright-colored costumes. As the dancers twirled and leapt, the chorus burst into song. Wow! It was spectacular! I soon found myself lost in the song, mouthing every word. It all looked so perfect—and then I noticed that something was wrong.

Part of the scenery was missing! A big section of the barn set hadn't made it onstage. Several of the dancers looked confused, but they tried to adjust by using the rest of the set to jump on and whirl around.

This was definitely a major problem. *Thank goodness I'm not out there,* I thought as I ran behind the backdrop to the other side of the stage. I discovered all the stagehands crowded around the missing section of the barn on its wheeled platform.

"What's going on?" I asked, standing on

tiptoe behind Trevor and trying to see over his shoulder.

"One of the brakes is jammed—we can't get the wheels moving, and this thing is too heavy to carry out there," he said without turning.

Molly came dancing off into the wings. "We can't do the next barn number without the rest of the set!" she wailed, panicked.

Trevor said, "We'll get it out there as soon as we can." Molly hurried back onstage. "They'll have to cut the dance if we can't get these wheels fixed," he mumbled as soon as she was out of earshot.

Penny came rushing over. "Trevor, what's the problem? Is it the wheels?"

He nodded. "If we can lift the platform slightly, maybe I could get under it and free the brake."

"Okay, everybody grab an edge," Penny said, hurrying over to one side of the platform. I followed the other stagehands, grabbing hold of the other side.

"No, Krista. Not you," Penny ordered. "We can handle this. You can't miss your cue. Colby's already upset enough about the set." I watched anxiously as they lifted and Trevor squeezed underneath, armed with a hammer and a wrench.

"I need a hand. Someone get down here!" Trevor's voice sounded urgent.

The stagehands looked at one another helplessly. They couldn't let go of the platform or Trevor would be crushed.

I glanced toward the stage. Scene two had already started. I was in the next one.

Without further thought I lay down on the floor and wriggled under the platform next to Trevor.

"Okay, hold this . . ." He handed me the hammer, then blinked. *"Krista?"*

"Everyone else is kinda tied up." I held the hammer while Trevor used the wrench. Then he took the hammer and used it to tap the locked brake until at last it released and the wheel spun free.

We slid out on our backs. Trevor and Alan began to move the piece into place, ready for the next scene change. Then Trevor turned and winked at me, sending a warm glow right through me. It felt like Trevor and I were a team again, only this time it was different somehow.

"Oh, no," Carol gasped as I moved into position for my entrance. "The back of your costume is filthy!" She tried to brush it off. "You can't wear this out there!"

I could hear scene two winding down. Inside I felt a surge of panic, but I forced myself to stay calm. I knew what I had to do, and took off in a mad dash for the dressing room.

There it was on the rack—the awful orange

dress. I quickly changed into it and bolted back upstairs. Penny gave me a little push, whispering, "You're on!"

I stumbled onto the brightly lit stage. I could see the surprised look on Jason's face when he saw the orange dress, but we went right into our scene without a hitch. I could feel the audience out there as if they were part of the scene, too—their anticipation, their laughter.

I made it through the scene without any trouble. In fact, I thought I'd done a pretty good job.

The minute we came offstage, Jason whispered, "What are you doing in that orange dress? Colby told you to wear the blue one."

"I had to help with the scenery, and the blue one got all dirty," I whispered back.

Jason looked disgusted. "Well, you should *not* have been working on the set in costume."

"But they needed my help," I said.

"So? That's *their* problem. Leave it to those clumsy peons to mess up!" He turned on his heel and went back onstage for the next scene.

I stared after him, amazed and angry. What a rotten thing to say! I couldn't *believe* him. He had such an attitude! We'd been working so hard to make sure the show ran smoothly, and Jason didn't care. All he cared about was the color of my dress! How could I have actually fallen for him?

I felt a warm hand on my shoulder. "Thanks, Krista. I . . . *we* really needed you." Trevor's voice was soft, and I could feel his breath close to my ear. It sent shivers through me, and so did his touch. Then the hand was gone, and so was Trevor.

The lights went down on scene four, and the crew set up scene five. My mind shifted gears, and I quickly ran through my lines in my head. This was my first scene with Trina. I knew I'd be okay if only she would leave me alone.

She didn't. On my first line, she crossed in front of me, blocking me from the audience. But I was getting used to that. It was like a game we were playing. I dodged from behind her and said my line loud and clear.

In the middle of the scene, she did it again. Only this time when I tried to move, she moved, too, and my knee slammed into the corner of a trunk. Pain shot up my leg. I quickly sank into the nearest chair. Reaching under the table, I rubbed my kneecap. It was throbbing something awful. I played the rest of the scene sitting at the table, thankful that at least the orange dress was partially hidden.

When the curtain closed for intermission, I started to hobble offstage just as Mr. Colby burst through the side door. He was really steamed. His face was contorted in an angry frown, and his fists were clenched. Everyone cleared a path for him—a path that led straight to me. I had no idea he'd be so angry about the orange dress. Maybe I should have worn the dirty blue one. . . .

But he stormed right past me. "Trina!" he yelled. "If I *ever* catch you pulling another stunt like that," he pointed right at me, "you will *never* work in this theater again! Is that understood?"

"Yes, sir," Trina said meekly, not meeting his eyes.

Mr. Colby turned to me. "Are you all right, Krista?"

I nodded. Before he could say anything about the orange dress, I explained. "I had to help with the scenery problem, and the blue dress got all messed up. This was my only choice." I held my breath. Would he understand?

"Thank you, Krista," he said with a smile. "Good work. And good thinking."

I let out a sigh of relief, glancing over at Jason. He just scowled and left. He wasn't turning out at *all* like I'd expected. Jason Stuart really wasn't a very nice person, I decided.

During intermission, I wanted to find Trevor, but Penny insisted on putting ice on my knee. I was glad she did, because the swelling went down, and I felt much better.

The second act went much more smoothly. The scenery all worked perfectly, and Trina left me alone so I could play my part without interference. Marcie didn't bother me, either—I guess she had gotten the message, too. During the scene changes, I watched Trevor move scenery and bring on props. It was hard to keep track of him—his black clothes blended in with the side curtains.

During the finale, I went through the motions, mouthing the lyrics as the others sang. I might have been onstage, but all my thoughts were backstage. What was Trevor doing? How was Trevor feeling? How did Trevor feel about *me*? When could we talk about everything? How had I missed seeing how perfect he was for me? I guess I had been blinded by the spotlight shining on the star of the show—Jason. But now I could see everything clearly, and the boy I really cared about wasn't in the spotlight, but somewhere behind the scenes.

When the curtain closed at the end of the show, the audience clapped and cheered. The curtain opened and closed six times before the applause died down. Then people began bringing flowers up onstage. There was a big bouquet of roses for Trina and one for Jason, and several bouquets for other key members of the cast.

There were even flowers for me! I saw Bobby climbing up the steps from the auditorium, almost hidden by the large bouquet of daisies he was carrying. I was afraid he was in trouble, and I was right. His toe caught on the last step. *Thunk!* Down went Bobby, and the daisies spilled all over the apron of the stage. The audience was in hysterics, but Bobby was almost in tears.

I rushed over to him and gave him a big hug. He hugged me back, then took off like a scared cat. Some of the other cast members helped me pick up the daisies from the floor while everybody laughed and clapped.

When the curtain closed for the final time, Sarah asked, "Was that your little brother? He's so cute!"

"Yeah, he's okay. But he's a bit of a spaz," I said with a smile, then hurried off, searching for Trevor. I didn't have much time—my parents would be waiting for me in the lobby. Checking the backstage area and the greenroom, I came up empty. Where was he? Was he still avoiding me? I would have to find him later, I thought as I ran into the lobby to meet my parents.

"Oh, Krista! You were *wonderful!*" Mo cried, throwing her arms around me.

My dad beamed with pride. "Good job, sweetie," he said.

I looked around for my brother. "Where's Bobby?" I asked.

Mo laughed. "Probably hiding. He was so embarrassed about the flowers. Bobby!" she called, and he slowly emerged from behind the water fountain.

"I'm sorry," he mumbled.

"Hey, you!" I went over to him and picked him up. "Thank you so much for the daisies. Did you pick them from our yard?"

He nodded, and a big smile spread across his face. "All of 'em. There's none left outside."

Remembering Trevor, I quickly set Bobby down. "Look, I gotta run. I have to talk to someone before the cast party."

"Okay, honey," Dad said. "Have fun and remember, be home by midnight."

"Sure thing." I ran into the auditorium. Maybe he was in there.

Trevor wasn't there, but Jason was. "Krista," he called to me. "You need a ride to the cast party?"

Yeah, right. Like I'd really want to go anywhere with him after the way he acted! "No, thanks," I said. "I have my own set of wheels, remember? Besides, I'm going with Trevor." That is, if I could find him and ask him and if he agreed.

Jason must have noticed my frosty tone, because he frowned. Then he motioned to a girl sitting in the front row. "Oh, I want you to meet someone. This is my girlfriend, Sharon. She's been away all summer." The tall girl came over to him and latched on to his arm.

"You did a nice job," she said, smiling.

I smiled, too. "Thanks." I was sure glad I'd come to my senses before I met Jason's girlfriend. It would have been stupid, getting heartbroken over such a jerk. I wondered what Sharon saw in him, aside from his stunning good looks. "Nice meeting you, Sharon. Bye!" I said. I just had to find Trevor.

I went up onto the stage and slipped between the curtains. Rodney was putting some of the props away. "Rodney, have you seen Trevor?" I asked.

"Try the greenroom—he was headed that way."

"Thanks!" A moment later, I burst into the greenroom, and there he was. "Trevor!" I cried. "I'm so glad I found you! I thought maybe we could go to the cast party together and talk or—or something. I miss talking to you so much, and I think we can be more than friends . . ." I wanted to tell him everything I'd been thinking for the past two hours, but he didn't give me a chance.

"Trouble in paradise?" he said, giving me a hurt, angry look. "Too bad Jason's girlfriend showed up, huh?" I started to speak, but he cut me off again. "Since you can't have him, I'm just supposed to sit here and be second choice. No thank you, Krista!" He turned and left the room.

I stood staring after him in shock. Now I knew what it meant to feel like you'd been hit with a ton of bricks. An unexpected tear trickled down my cheek, and I brushed it away. I'd thought everything was going to be so great, and now it was all falling apart.

"Krista, can I hitch a ride with you to the cast party?" I heard Carol's voice behind me.

I shook my head. "I'm not going," I said without turning. "I'm not feeling very well." Carol didn't say anything. She just left. All I wanted was to get away from there, to go someplace where no one would find me.

Chapter Ten

I parked my truck on the street outside my house a few minutes later. Home was the last place I wanted to go, but I simply couldn't think of anywhere else to hide. Leaning my forehead on the steering wheel, I felt hot tears sting my cheeks. This was definitely the worst night of my life.

The porch light was on, but I knew my folks didn't expect me home for a couple of hours. To avoid questions, I slipped through the gate into the backyard, and let myself in the back door. I tiptoed up the stairs to my room and threw myself on the bed. If only Trevor would give me a chance! If we could only talk things out, I was sure I could explain everything.

I had half a notion to look up his number

in the phone book and call—I knew he lived on Warner Boulevard. But that would be dumb. He'd be at the party, and even if he stopped by his house beforehand, he'd probably hang up on me. The thought gave me a sick, empty feeling in my stomach. A few leftover tears ran down my cheeks. There was absolutely nothing I could do. I rolled over, grabbed a pen and notepad from my nightstand, and began to write:

Dear Beth,

I've really blown it this time. You were right, Trevor was the guy for me. I was just too stupid to realize it until it was too late. Now he won't even talk to me. He thinks the only reason I like him is because Jason has a girlfriend, which isn't true. I decided he was the one I liked before I knew about Jason's girl. Now I've lost Trevor for good. I don't blame him for being mad—he thinks he's just second choice. But I really care about him, Beth, and now there's nothing I can do. . . .

Another tear escaped and dripped onto the letter, blurring the ink. I would have to finish it later. Putting my notepad back on the table, I headed into the bathroom. I thought

I might feel better if I washed my face. Maybe I could wash away the tears. But it didn't work. I climbed into bed without bothering to change my clothes. Turning off the lamp, I pulled the covers over my head. Even though the show had been a success, my night was a total disaster.

When I opened my eyes, the morning sun was peeking in through the blinds. Stretching and yawning, I rolled over and checked the clock. It was already ten o'clock. I was feeling pretty good—until I remembered last night. With a groan, I decided it would be better not to get up at all. I had sure messed up yesterday. "Forget it, it's all over," I kept telling myself, but one little part of me just wasn't listening. I think it was my heart.

An hour later, I forced myself to face what was left of the morning. It was a beautiful day, so I might as well try to enjoy it.

I took off the rumpled clothes I had slept in, put on a T-shirt and shorts, and went slowly downstairs. As I walked into the kitchen, Mo stood up and began to clap. "Bravo! Bravo! A star is born!" she said, smiling.

I took a quick bow and tried to smile back.

Bobby came running in. "Krista, you were *so* good! I told all my friends that you were in a play, and that I saw you." He wore a grin that stretched from ear to ear. The little demon could be so nice sometimes, it made me forget his rotten days—well, almost.

"Thanks, Bobby." I gave him a high-five, and he exited the kitchen at top speed.

"He's been so excited, but I wouldn't let him wake you," Mo said. "You don't have to go to the theater today, do you?"

"No, we have today off, and then we go back to clean up and tear down the set."

She raised her eyebrow at the last comment.

"No, we don't actually rip it up," I explained. "It's a theater term for taking it apart."

"So how was the cast party?" Mo asked.

I had been dreading this question. "Okay, I guess," I hedged. I didn't want to tell her that I hadn't gone, and why. She'd just be full of more questions and motherly advice. But I felt terrible about not telling her the truth.

"Did you have a good time?" Mo persisted.

Instead of answering, I went over and peered into the refrigerator. "Do we have anything to eat?"

"Just the usual." She sounded a little disappointed that I didn't go into detail about the party, but I was grateful that she didn't pursue the subject.

The doorbell rang, and I heard Bobby run

to open it. Then he catapulted into the kitchen. "Krista, you have a visitor!"

"Who is it?" I asked, trying to smooth my tangled hair.

"I'm not supposed to tell," he said with a smirk and then disappeared out the back door.

My heart leapt. Could it be Trevor? Had he changed his mind about me? I tried to walk calmly to the front door, fixing my messy hair as best I could.

The door burst open. "Surprise!"

"Beth!" I shrieked in amazement.

"I got sent home early—they didn't need me for the second session." We gave each other a big hug.

"So, are you glad to see me?" she said, letting me go.

"I sure am." And I was, but I found it hard to smile.

Beth looked at me closely. "Then why do you look so bummed? What's going on, Krista?"

"I kinda screwed things up at the theater," I mumbled.

"With your job?"

"No . . ." A tear slipped out before I could blink it back.

Her voice softened. "Tell me what happened. Is it Jason?"

I shook my head. "No," I choked. "Trevor."

"Trevor?" Beth looked confused.

I led the way to my room, where I silently ripped the letter off my notepad and handed it to her. After taking a minute to read it, she gave me another hug. "Maybe we can work this out."

I wiped my eyes. "No. It's too late. I've already ruined everything. He doesn't like me anymore. In fact, I think he *hates* me!"

"Come on, let's go outside," Beth suggested. "The sun will make you feel better." She smiled, one of those warm, caring Beth-smiles that I had missed so much.

It was wonderful to have my best friend back. Now I had someone to share all my feelings with, someone who really understood. If only Beth could help me figure out some way to fix everything with Trevor. If only I could go back in time to that night on the stage when we had drunk sparkling cider, and Trevor had kissed me! But no—I'd blown that one as well.

We went downstairs and out into the backyard. The sun did feel good. I hadn't seen much of it all summer, but Beth looked fantastic with her bronze tan. While we basked, she filled me in on everything about camp— the kids, the activities, the food, and the pranks. And then it was my turn. I spilled out all the details about Trevor, Jason, the theater, the picnic, my part, and last night.

It felt so good to get it off my chest, and Beth understood just how I was feeling, as I had known she would.

"What you need, Krista, is to stop sitting around moping," she said. "Get out and *do* something. I have to run a few errands for my mom, but why don't we meet for lunch at Kadie's diner in about an hour?"

"Sounds good," I agreed.

"Okay, I'll catch you later." Beth waved as she left through the back gate.

I love Kadie's. The diner is decorated fifties style. They have an old-fashioned soda fountain, and the opposite wall is lined with big red vinyl booths. An old jukebox stands in the corner, and the thing still works. Seeing that Beth hadn't arrived when I got there, I went over to check out the songs on the jukebox.

I scanned the play list: "Heartbreak Hotel," "Bye-Bye Love," "Long, Lonely Nights" . . . Maybe music wasn't such a great idea after all. I finally selected a couple of numbers by the Beach Boys, dropped in my quarters, and slid into a booth to wait for Beth. After I had listened to both songs, I checked my watch. Almost twenty past one. Where was she? There was a big picture of a strawberry float propped up against the napkin dispenser. My stomach started to grumble.

A waitress came over to my table with her pad and pencil. "Can I get you anything?"

I shook my head. "Not yet. I'm waiting for my friend."

"Okay. Just give me a holler when you're ready," she said with a pleasant smile, and went to wait on some of the other customers.

I stared at the picture of the strawberry float. It was bright pink in a huge glass, topped with a mound of whipped cream and a giant strawberry. My stomach growled even louder.

"Waiting for someone?" a boy's voice said. I tore my eyes away from the strawberry float, and gasped. It was Trevor! "Um . . . well . . . yeah," I stammered.

He smiled as he slid into the booth opposite me. "Surprised to see me?"

I nodded wordlessly, unable to think of anything intelligent to say. What was he doing here? I mean, I was glad he was, but how . . . why . . . ?

"Beth said she couldn't make it," he said, taking a piece of paper out of his jeans pocket. As he unfolded it, I recognized it immediately. It was the letter I'd given Beth! Part of me wanted to hug her, and the other half wanted to punch her for sharing my private note with Trevor. I could feel my face turning beet-red.

He raised his eyes to mine. "I got a little unexpected mail at home today." He paused and then went on, "I know you didn't mean for me to see this, Krista, but I'm glad I did, or else I wouldn't have known how you felt about everything." Trevor's green eyes sparkled as they held mine. "I guess it's not all that surprising that those of us behind the scenes get lost, compared to the guys onstage in the bright lights and fancy costumes," he said softly.

"I'm sorry," I whispered. "I . . ."

"It's okay," he said, taking my hand across the table. His hand was so big and warm. My fingers tingled.

"But I was such a . . ." I began.

"Shhh," Trevor said. "It doesn't matter anymore. The play is over. That scene is finished. But you and me—well, we're just starting."

I squeezed his fingers lightly. "Thanks for being so understanding, so wonderful . . ."

"So are you two ready to order?" The waitress was back.

She had caught me a little off guard. "Ummm . . ." I glanced longingly at the strawberry float, then opened the menu.

Trevor grinned at me, and pointed at the picture of the float. "We'll start with one of these. Two straws, please," he told the waitress.

"We're on the same wavelength," I laughed, closing the menu.

Trevor shrugged. "I could have told you that from day one."

I felt something pressing against my foot under the table. Was it Trevor, or another embarrassing table leg? Instead of looking, I gave it a little kick.

"Ow!" Trevor said in mock pain.

Good! It's alive! I thought, and said aloud, "Sorry." I smiled and moved my foot closer to his.

When the waitress set the big fluffy pink float on the table between us, she gave Trevor a wink as she handed him the two straws. "Have fun."

"Here you go." Trevor poked the straws into the float. "He—or she—who slurps the fastest gets the most." We both laughed. It felt good to laugh with Trevor again! It hadn't happened in so long. Why had I been so slow to figure out that he was boyfriend material?

Trevor had already begun to attack the float, so I quickly captured my straw. Our heads were so close together that I could feel his curls tickling my forehead. My stomach did a little flip, and I giggled.

"What?" he said, raising his head. Our noses touched, and a little thrill ran through me. No wonder Eskimos kissed with their noses!

"Nothing," I said, giggling again.

By the time we finished the float, I was stuffed, probably mostly with happiness.

"Want anything else?" Trevor asked.

You, I wanted to say, but I just shook my head.

Trevor took out a five-dollar bill and put it on the table.

"Oh, I have money," I said, reaching for my wallet.

"My treat." Trevor winked at me as we slid out of the booth.

I didn't argue. I guess this would qualify as our first date.

The jukebox was blaring with Chubby Checker singing, "Oh, baby, let's do the twist . . ." As if on cue, Trevor grabbed my hand and we both started twisting toward the door.

Outside, we burst into laughter. "Maybe we were born in the wrong era," Trevor suggested. "You'd look good in a poodle skirt and bobby socks."

"You'd look good in just about anything," I said.

Trevor smiled. "You think so?"

I blushed. "Well, yeah. I mean, a guy who looks good in black can wear anything."

He draped an arm around my shoulder. "You look pretty good in black yourself." He let his arm slip down, and grabbed my hand. Lacing his fingers with mine, he swung our hands gently as we walked along the sidewalk.

After all that had happened between us, I'd never thought Trevor would hold my hand, or that I would feel so happy.

When we reached his car, we stopped. Was he going to kiss me? I wondered. If he did, this time it would be different—*much* different. This time I *wanted* him to kiss me. He looked down at me and smiled. My heart was pounding a hundred beats a second, and I started to get nervous. Well, was he or wasn't he? Maybe after the last time, he wouldn't dare to kiss me again.

Trevor let go of my hand, and my heart sank. He wasn't going to kiss me. Instead, he opened the hood of his bug, which was parked in front of my truck, and pulled out the jumper cables.

"Guess what I need?" he said as he walked over to me.

"A jump?" I said halfheartedly.

"No, but that was a good guess." He took the cables and wrapped them around me, pulling me close. When he leaned over and gently kissed my lips, I felt tingly all over and my knees went weak. Thank goodness for those cables, or I probably would have collapsed on the pavement!

Opening my eyes, I saw Trevor smiling at

me. "How about an encore?" he asked. This time I was ready and kissed him back. It was like we had left the planet and were floating together in space.

As the jumper cables fell to our feet, Trevor replaced them with his arms. I had found my leading man, and I was sure our romance would have a long, long run.

Sweet Dreams

SWEET DREAMS are fresh, fun and exciting —alive with the flavor of the contemporary teen scene—the joy and doubt of first love. If you've missed any SWEET DREAMS titles, then you're missing out on your kind of stories, written about people like you!